Jerry McAuley

His Life and Work

Jerry McAuley

His Life and Work

ISBN/EAN: 9783743370951

Manufactured in Europe, USA, Canada, Australia, Japa

Cover: Foto ©Raphael Reischuk / pixelio.de

Manufactured and distributed by brebook publishing software (www.brebook.com)

Jerry McAuley

His Life and Work

JERRY McAULEY.

His Life and Work

WITH

INTRODUCTION

BY THE REV. S. IRENÆUS PRIME, D.D.

AND

PERSONAL SKETCHES

BY A. S. HATCH, ESQ.

EDITED BY REV. R. M. OFFORD

SECOND EDITION

NEW YORK
PUBLISHED BY THE NEW YORK OBSERVER
37 AND 38 PARK ROW

PREFACE.

DURING the summer preceding his death Jerry McAuley was planning for the preparation of a somewhat extensive account of God's dealings with and through him. He purposed waiting only for cooler weather before commencing his task. But his death intervened ere the work had even been begun. We have thus been deprived of many of the records of the richest displays of God's grace in both the Water Street and the Cremorne Missions. But enough have been printed in the following pages to arouse the deepest interest of Christian hearts. These records serve to show that, in the dispensation of grace and graces, God is no respecter of persons. As in nature the most resplendent gems are found among the most uninviting surroundings, so grace gathers out of the horrible pit and the miry clay many a bright gem for the Saviour's diadem. And God works through lowly instrumentalities. In this respect his choice is often contrary to human judgment. Jerry was a very unpromising sinner to begin with, but God in His grace saved him. After his conversion he seemed by no means a promising saint, and ministers and others engaged in mission work did not encourage him to believe that he was called to labor in that direction. But God had called him none the less, and owned and blessed him beyond all human conception or computation. It is indeed true that we have this treasure in earthen vessels, that the glory may be the Lord's.

It is fitting that acknowledgments be made here of indebtedness to those friends who have helped to produce this volume. The first three chapters are taken from the little work "Transformed," edited by Mrs. Helen E. Brown. Three of the later chapters are devoted to personal recollections of the worker and his work, by A. S. Hatch, Esq. There are no more interesting chapters in the book than these, and they greatly enhance its value. That gentleman has placed us under further obligations by the care and patience with which he has read every line of this volume, revising where necessary—a task which his long and intimate acquaintance with Jerry enabled him to do better than any one else could have done it. To the Rev. S. Irenæus Prime, D.D., thanks are due for the "Introduction." His reminiscences of Jerry, couched in such tender and touching language, will serve to awaken at the start a deep interest in the records which follow.

My own part of the work has been a very modest one. Collecting such material as already existed, and which best served to present Jerry the outcast, Jerry the transformed, Jerry the successful worker for souls, the matter has been prepared for the printer without any attempt to give the facts in any setting of beautiful language. The labor has been a simple but very pleasant one. To have helped in any way to publish the story of grace as it triumphed in and through Jerry McAuley is an honor greatly esteemed, and for which the heart feels sincerely grateful to God. It is indeed to be wished that He may be glorified in the record as He was in its subject.

May Christians who read these pages be encouraged to

work for the salvation of the most outcast of their fellow-beings! May many of those who are as yet unsaved be led by these records to seek Jerry McAuley's Saviour, the Lord Jesus Christ. Of that blessed Redeemer it is written in God's Book, the Bible, " He is able also to save them to the uttermost that come unto God by him, seeing he ever liveth to make intercession for them" (Heb. vii. 25). His own words are : " Come unto Me, all ye that labor and are heavy laden, and I will give you rest " (Matt. xi. 28).

THE EDITOR.

PREFACE TO SECOND EDITION.

WITH gratitude to God record is here made that the first edition of this work has been abundantly owned and blessed of Him. The second and still larger edition is sent out with prayers as fervent and hopes as ardent as those which accompanied the first. May every copy carry a blessing!

CONTENTS.

INTRODUCTION.

BY REV. S. IRENÆUS PRIME, D.D.

RETURNING home after my summer recess in 1884, I had not been in my house five minutes when a gentleman called to ask me to conduct the funeral of Jerry McAuley.

. "Is he dead?" I asked in a burst of mingled surprise and sorrow. Before going away I had seen and heard the manifest, signs of consumption, and it was not wonderful that such a life as he led in the days of his wickedness should make him an easy prey to disease. He did not live out half his days, though grace did come to the everlasting life of his soul.

But it made me very sad. I did not know that this strange man had such a place in my heart that now he was dead I should feel as if the city and the world and I had lost a friend. Jerry is dead! Well, what was he to me that I must grieve that I shall see his face no more? He came often to see me, and said little when he was there, but seemed to love to sit near me, and look up with a tearful eye and a pensive face, and a heart, I doubt not, full of sweet hope and holy love. We never talked of the old, old times when he was a thief and a robber, when he was a drunkard and blasphemer, when he was a convict in prison, and afterwards an outcast and an outlaw. It is not in my memory that a word ever passed between us about those terrible days and nights of sin and shame, when he won distinction among the criminal classes as one of the worst of men, a dangerous character, unfit to be at large—as unfit to live as he was unprepared to die. It has always been a marvel to me that men professing to be reformed from loathsome habits should revel in the recital of their past sins, as if they were heroes who had come out of a great battle, and were now victors to be crowned and counted worthy of honor. Jerry McAuley was not so. He kept in mind the pit from which he was dug, but the memory of it filled him with penitence and pain. He would speak of it when the fact of his rescue would help a perishing brother to struggle for deliverance; but he loved rather when with me to speak of the life that he now lived—"yet not I, but Christ liveth in me: I live by the faith of the Son of God, who loved me, and gave himself for me." Delivered from the powers of darkness and translated into the kingdom of God's dear Son, this poor sinner, clothed and in his right mind, had put away the old man with his lusts, and now a new man in Christ Jesus was striving to walk humbly and softly before God. He never seemed confident that he might not be delivered again into the hand of Satan, to be buffeted for a season; but he sought sustaining grace and found it day by day, till the convicted sinner was transformed into a redeemed soul by the Spirit of God and the victory of the grave.

The next day was the Sabbath. The funeral was to be in the afternoon. As the hour approached—and indeed all the day—my thoughts had been dwelling on the fact that

New York has no consciousness of the loss it has met: the city knows not that one of the most useful men in it, one of its most remarkable, wonderful men, is to be buried to-day. Very few know or care about Jerry McAuley; we are going to the Broadway Tabernacle to talk of what he was and what he has done, to a little congregation that will gather there: if it were Dr. Taylor, the beloved and honored pastor, the house would be crowded and the mourners would go about the streets; but poor Jerry—he is dead, and who will be there to weep with us over his remains? Ah, how little did I know the place that he filled in the heart of this vast city! I was to conduct the funeral, and went early to complete the arrangements. As I turned down from the Fifth Avenue through Thirty-fourth Street, I saw a vast multitude standing in the sunshine, filling the streets and the square in front of the Tabernacle. Astonished at the spectacle, and wondering they did not go and take seats in the church, I soon found that the house was packed with people so that it was impossible for me to get within the door. Proclamation was made that the clergy who were to officiate were on the outside, and a passage was made for them to enter in. What could be more impressive and expressive of the estimate set upon the man and his work! There is no other Christian worker in the city who would have called out these uncounted thousands in a last tribute of love and honor of his memory. And then eloquent lips spoke of him and the great good done by him in fields of labor uninviting, and often repelling those who care for the souls of the perishing among us. It was said that there is no one pastor in New York who is doing the work of this humble man —no pastor who will leave a wider vacancy when he falls on the high places in his field of duty.

To read the story of his life and work is not like the romance born of a lively fancy, for it is far more strange, unreal, *incredible*, than the novel of the period. It involves the supernatural. It has to do directly with the powers of the world to come. Reading it, still more going into one of the meetings where lost men and women come to be saved, brings one at once into the midst of agencies that imply for their power and success the immediate, direct, personal presence and working influence of the Holy Spirit. If this work is not of God, it is nothing; worse than nothing—it is an awful farce. To me it is a divine reality. It was no fanaticism that in the days of the apostles led men to cry out "What must I do to be saved;" and when I have sat in the midst of publicans and harlots, convicts and thieves, drunkards and other vile and wretched human beings down so low in misery and shame that no human arm is long enough to reach them or strong enough to raise and save them; when I have heard them in broken accents, amid sobs and tears, tell what the grace of God has done for them, how it had brought husbands and wives together in peace and comfort, with happy children around them, after liquor and crime and gaunt want had broken up the household; when I have heard scores and scores of such testimonies ascribing all their salvation to Him who loved them and died for them, lost and ruined by sin—the tears have run down like rivers of waters from mine eyes, and I have prayed that hundreds and thousands of preachers of righteousness like Jerry McAuley might be taken from prison to go in the name of Jesus to seek and to save them that are lost.

It is a good thing to write and print and spread the life of such a man as the hero of this volume. It may kindle the flame in many other hearts. Christians in other walks of life than he trod may be stirred to better living. And (may God in infinite mercy grant it!) some poor, sinning soul, some wretched and sinking soul, some poor sinner, almost as bad as Jerry was, may read it in his extremity, and cry out with this ransomed prisoner, "Lord save me, I perish."

To

MARIA,

THE WELL BELOVED AND LOVING WIFE AND TRUE HELPMEET, WHO FAITHFULLY LABORED
SIDE BY SIDE WITH JERRY, SHARING ALL THE TRIALS AND TRIUMPHS OF
HIS REDEEMED LIFE, AND WHO BRAVELY TOOK UP HIS
WORK WHERE HE LAID IT DOWN, WHEN
THE LORD CALLED HIM HOME,

This volume is respectfully dedicated by

THE EDITOR.

JERRY MCAULEY.

CHAPTER I.

TRANSFORMED.

"Our young life had dark beginning,
  Helpless and alone we lay;
Knowing only sin and sorrow,
  Till the Saviour passed that way."

THE following autobiographical sketch of Jerry McAuley and the beginning of his Christian work was written in 1875, mainly from Jerry's dictation, and was widely circulated and read at the time, under the title of "Transformed; or, The History of a River Thief." With a careful revision, and with some additional facts relating to the early part of Jerry's redeemed life and the origin of the Mission in Water Street, supplied in their proper connection by a loving hand, it is here reproduced as the most fitting introduction to the present volume.

I do not attempt this record of my life from any feeling of vain-glory, or any craving for notoriety. Neither is it because I have had a remarkable history. I have been a great sinner, and have found Jesus a great Saviour; and this is why I would tell my story, that others may be led to adore and seek the blessed Friend who saved, and has thus far kept me by his grace.

I was born in Ireland. Our family was broken up by sin, for my father was a counterfeiter, and left home to escape the law, before I knew him. I was placed at a very early age in the family of my grandmother, who was a devout Romanist. My first recollections of her are of her counting her beads, and kissing the floor for penance. I would take the opportunity while she was prostrated upon her face, to throw things at her head, in my mischievous play, and when she rose from her knees, it was to curse and swear at me. At such times I can distinctly remember thinking, though I could not have formed the thought into words, "What sort of religion is this that requires such foolish worship, and allows such sinful ways?" I can trace my infidelity to Rome to just these incidents.

I was never taught or sent to school, but left to have my own way; to roam about in idleness, doing mischief continually, and suffering from the cruel and harsh treatment of those who had the care of me.

At the age of thirteen I was sent to this country, to the care of a married sister in New York City. Here I ran errands in the family, and assisted my brother-in-law in his business, and soon, by the practice of little tricks, became well used to dishonesty, and was as great a rogue as one of my years could be. After a while I felt I could live by my own wits, and left my sister's home to take care of myself. I took board in a family in Water Street, where were two young men with whom I associated myself in business. I earned what I could, and stole the rest, to supply my daily wants.

We had a boat, by means of which we boarded vessels

in the night, stealing whatever we could lay our hands on. Here I began my career as a river-thief. In the daytime we went up into the city and sold our ill-gotten goods, and with the proceeds dressed up, and then spent our time, as long as our money lasted, in the vile dens of Water Street, practising all sorts of wickedness. Here I learned to be a prize-fighter, and by degrees, rapid degrees, rose through all the grades of vice and crime, till I became a terror and nuisance in the Fourth Ward.

I was only nineteen years of age when I was arrested for highway robbery—a child in years, but a man in sin. I knew nothing of the criminal act which was charged to my account; but the rumsellers and inhabitants of the Fourth Ward hated me for all my evil ways, and were glad to get rid of me. So they swore the robbery on me, and I couldn't help myself. I had no friends, no advocate at court (it is a bad thing, sinners, not to have an advocate at court), and without any just cause I was sentenced to fifteen years in State prison. I burned with vengeance; but what could I do? I was handcuffed, and sent in the cars to Sing-Sing.

That ride was the saddest hour of my life. I looked back on my whole past course, on all my hardships, my misery and sins, and gladly would I have thrown myself out before the advancing train, and ended my life. It was not sorrow for sin that possessed me, but a heavy weight seemed to press me down when I thought of the punishment I had got to suffer for my wrong-doings, and an indignant, revengeful feeling for the injustice of my sentence. Fifteen years of hard labor in a prison to look forward to, and all for a crime I was as innocent of as the babe unborn. I knew I had done enough to condemn me,

if it were known ; but others, as bad as I, were at liberty,
and I was suffering the penalty for one who was at that
hour roaming at will, glorying in his lucky escape from
punishment, and caring nothing for the unhappy dog who
was bearing it in his stead. How my heart swelled with
rage, and then sank like lead, as I thought of my helpless-
ness in the hands of the law, without a friend in the world.

I concluded, however, before I reached the end of that
short journey, that my best way was to be obedient to
prison rules, do the best I could under the circumstances,
and trust that somebody would be raised up to help me.

When I arrived at the prison—I shall never forget it—
the first thing that attracted my attention was the sentence
over the door: " The way of transgressors is hard." Though
I could not read very well, I managed to spell that out. It
was a familiar sentence, which I had heard a great many
times. All thieves and wicked people know it well, and
they know, too, that it is out of the Bible. It is a well-
worn proverb in all the haunts of vice, and one confirmed
by daily experience. And how strange it is that, knowing
so well that the way is hard, the transgressors will still go
in it.

But God was more merciful to me than man. His pure
eyes had seen all my sin, and yet he pitied and loved me,
and stretched out his hand to save me. And his wonderful
way of doing it was to shut me up in a cell within those
heavy stone walls. There's many a one beside me who
will have cause to thank God for ever and ever that he
was shut up in a prison.

I was put to the carpet-weaving business, and for two
years not a word could be said against me. All the keepers
and guards spoke well of me. I minded my work, and was

quiet and orderly. I used to say my prayer—the Lord's
Prayer—every day, from a feeling that it was right to say it,
and that in some way or other it would do me good. I
tried to learn to read and write, and improved very much,
more especially in reading. Then I got cheap novels and
read, to pass away the time. I read many and many of
them. It was all the recreation I had, and diverted my mind
from my dreary surroundings. I was supplied with them
constantly, and, in consequence, my head was filled with
low and wicked thoughts. I took a fancy, from some of
the remarkable stories I read, that I might by some good
fortune by and by effect my escape from the prison, and then
my heart would fill up with murderous intentions toward
the man who put me in.

After this I was sick, and suffered a good deal for two or
three years, and became at times uneasy and intractable.
Then I had to suffer severe punishment; but punishment
never did me a particle of good, it only made me harder
and harder.

I had been in the prison four or five years, when, one Sunday morning, I went with the rest to service in the chapel.
I was moody and miserable. As I took my seat, I raised my
eyes carelessly to the platform, and who should I see there
beside the chaplain but a man named Orville Gardner, who
had been for years a confederate in sin. "Awful Gardner"
was the name by which I had always known him. Since
my imprisonment he had been converted, and was filled
with desire to come to the prison, that he might tell the
glad story to the prisoners. I had not heard he was coming, and could not have been more surprised if an angel
had come down from heaven. I knew him at the first
glance, although he was so greatly changed from his old

rough dress and appearance. After the first look I began
to question in my mind if it was he after all, and thought I
must be mistaken ; but the moment he spoke I was sure,
and my attention was held fast.

He said he did not feel that he belonged on the platform,
where the ministers of God and good men stood to preach
the gospel to the prisoners; he was not worthy of such a
place. So he came down and stood on the floor in front of
the desk, that he might be among the men. He told them
it was only a little while since he had taken off the stripes
which they were then wearing ; and while he was talking
his tears fairly rained down out of his eyes. Then he knelt
down and prayed, and sobbed and cried, till I do not believe
there was a dry eye in the whole crowd. Tears filled my
eyes, and I raised my hand slowly to wipe them off, for I
was ashamed to have my companions or the guards see me
weep; but how I wished I was alone, or that it was dark,
that I might give way to my feelings unobserved. I knew
this man was no hypocrite. We had been associated in
many a dark deed and sinful pleasure. I had heard oaths
and curses, vile and angry words from his mouth, and I
knew he could not talk as he did then unless some great,
wonderful change had come to him. I devoured every word
that fell from his lips, though I could not understand half
I heard. One sentence, however, impressed me deeply,
which he said was a verse from the Bible. The Bible!
I knew there was such a book, that people pretended
it was a message from God ; but I had never cared for it,
or read a word in it. But now God's time had come, and
he was going to show me the treasures that were hid in that
precious book.

I went back to my cell. How dreary is Sunday in prison !

After the morning service in the chapel, the prisoners are marched back to their cells, taking their plate of dinner with them as they pass the dining-hall, and the rest of the day is spent in solitude. Oh, those long, dismal hours! I had generally contrived to have a novel on hand, but that day I had none. What I had heard was ringing in my ears, and the thought possessed me to find the verse which had so struck me. Every prison-cell is supplied with a Bible; but, alas! few of them are used. Mine I had never touched since the day I entered my narrow apartment, and laid it away in the ventilator. I took it down, beat the dust from it, and opened it. But where to turn to find the words I wanted I knew not. There was nothing to do but to begin at the beginning, and read till I came to them. On and on I read. How interested I grew! It seemed better than any novel I had ever read, and I could scarcely leave it to go to sleep. I become so fascinated, that from that day on it was my greatest delight. I was glad when I was released from work, that I might get hold of my Bible; and night after night, when daylight was gone, I stood up by my grated door to read by the dim light which came from the corridor. I had supposed it to be a dry, dead thing—a book only fit for priests and saints, but now, whenever I could get a chance to communicate with my mates in the workshop, I told them that it was a "splendid thing, that Bible."

I never found that verse. I had forgotten it in my new interest in the book. But I found a good many verses that made me stop and think. At last I came to first Timothy, fourth chapter, which begins in this way: " Now the Spirit speaketh expressly, that in the latter times some shall depart from the faith, giving heed to seducing spirits, and

doctrines of devils; speaking lies in hypocrisy; having
their conscience seared with a hot iron ; forbidding to
marry, and commanding to abstain from meats, which God
hath created to be received with thanksgiving of them
which believe and know the truth." I threw down the
book, and kicked it about my cell. "The vile heretics," I
cried; "there's their lies. I always heard the old book was
a pack of lies. That's the way they hold us Catholics up."

Something seemed to whisper to me, "Go get a Catholic
Bible, and then you can prove this to be false." I couldn't
get rid of the thought. I took my first chance to go to the
library and ask for a Catholic Bible. They looked at me
pretty sharp, as though they would like to understand what
I was driving at; but they gave me what I wanted, and I
took it to my cell. Eagerly I turned to that chapter.
There they were, the very same words, "forbidding to
marry," and "commanding to abstain from meats." But
there were notes in the margin, which boxed it up so, that
my suspicions were at once aroused. I said, "It surely is
the Word of God, and they are trying to get out of it." I
turned to various parts, to Kings, Isaiah, and other books,
and I found that the words in both were almost the same,
the meaning was the same always, and I was in despair.
Then I read the whole book through again, and liked it
better the second time than I did the first. The book of
Revelation particularly astonished me. I tried to believe,
but I could not understand it.

I was resting one night from reading, walking up and
down and thinking what a change religion had made in
Gardner, when I began to have a burning desire to have the
same. I could not get rid of it: but what could I do?
Something within me said "Pray." I couldn't frame a

prayer. The voice said, "Don't you remember the prayer of the publican, 'God be merciful to me a sinner'?" I thought of my own religion, the Roman Catholic faith, in which I had been brought up, and I asked, "Why can't I be good in that?" "But that will not save me as Gardner's does him," I thought; "it does not keep me free from my sins." There was a struggle in my mind. "If I send for the priest," I said to myself, "he will tell me I must do penance, say so many prayers, and do something for mortification, and such as that. If I ask the chaplain, he will tell me to be sorry for my sins, and cry to God for forgiveness. Both can't be right." The voice within said, "Go to God; He will tell you what is right."

What a struggle I went through! I knew I ought to pray; but if there had been ten thousand people there I couldn't have been more ashamed to do it than I was there all alone. I felt myself blushing. Every sin stared me in the face. I recollected the "Whosoever" in the Bible. "That means you," said the inward voice. "But I'm so wicked," I urged; "everything but a murderer, and that many a time in my will." The struggle did not seem all my own; it was as if God was fighting the devil for me. To every thought that came up there came a verse of the Scripture. I fell on my knees, and was so ashamed I jumped up again. I fell on my knees again, and cried out for help, and then, as ashamed as before, I rose again. I put it off for that time and went to bed.

This conflict went on for three or four weeks. It was fearful. I wonder now at the long-suffering mercy of my God. I wonder that the Holy Spirit was not grieved to depart from me forever. But at last the Lord sent a softness and tenderness into my soul, and I shed many tears. Then

2

I cried unto the Lord, and began to read the Bible on my
knees.

The Sunday services seemed to do me no good. They
were dry and dead to me. Once in a while a man full of
the Holy Ghost preached for us, and at such times I got a
little help. About that date Miss D—— began to visit the
prison, and I was sent for one day to meet her in the
library. This young lady had learned that I was seeking
the Saviour, and had asked to see me. She talked with me,
and then knelt down to pray. I felt ashamed, but I knelt
beside her. I looked through my fingers and watched her.
I saw her tears fall. An awe I cannot describe fell on me.
It seemed dreadful to me, the prayer of that holy woman.
It made my sins rise up till they looked to me as if they
rose clean up to the throne of God, and it appeared to me
as if they troubled God, they rose up so high. What should
I do? Oh, what can a poor sinner do when there is nothing
between him and God but a life of dark, terrible sin?

That night I fell on my knees on the hard stone-floor of
my cell, resolved to stay there, whatever might happen, till
I found forgiveness. I was desperate. I felt just like the
words of the hymn,

> "Perhaps he will admit my plea,
>   Perhaps will hear my prayer,
> But if I perish I will pray,
>   And perish only there."

I prayed, and then I stopped; I prayed again, and
stopped; but still I continued kneeling. My knees were
rooted to those cold stones. My eyes were closed, and my
hands tightly clasped, and I was determined I would stay
so till morning, till I was called to my work; "and then,"

said I to myself, "if I get no relief, I will never, never pray again." I felt that I might die, but I didn't care for that.

All at once it seemed as if something supernatural was in my room. I was afraid to open my eyes. I was in an agony, and the sweat rolled off my face in great drops. Oh, how I longed for God's mercy! Just then, in the very height of my distress, it seemed as if a hand was laid upon my head, and these words came to me: "My son, thy sins, which are many, are forgiven." I do not know if I heard a voice, yet the words were distinctly spoken to my soul. Oh, the precious Christ! How plainly I saw him, lifted on the cross for my sins! What a thrill went through me. I jumped from my knees; I paced up and down my cell. A heavenly light seemed to fill it; a softness and a perfume like the fragrance of sweetest flowers. I did not know if I was living or not. I clapped my hands and shouted, "Praise God! Praise God!"

One of the guards was passing along the corridor, and called out, "What's the matter?" "I've found Christ," I answered; "my sins are all forgiven. Glory to God!" He took out a paper from his pocket and wrote the number of my cell, and threatened to report me in the morning. But I didn't care for that. My soul was all taken up with my great joy. But the next morning nothing happened to me, and I think the Lord made him forget it. What a night that was! I shall surely never forget the time when the Lord appeared as my gracious Deliverer from sin.

CHAPTER II.

STRUGGLES AND TEMPTATIONS.

" In the way a thousand snares
Lie, to take us unawares.
Satan, with malicious art,
Watches each unguarded part."

FROM that time life was all new to me. Work was
nothing; hard fare nothing; scowls and harsh words
nothing. I was happy, for Jesus was my friend; my sins
were washed away, and my heart was full of love and
thanksgiving. I hated every sinful way. I had formerly
smoked, but something within now said it was wrong, and
I gave it up.

And the Lord began to use me in the prison among my
fellow-convicts. A great work was commenced there, and
spread from cell to cell. The prisoners began to read their
Bibles, to call upon God, and to praise the name of Jesus.

Jack Dare was the first man I began to pray for. There
had been a revolt in the prison, and he was one of the
leaders. This revolt occurred some time before my conversion, but I had no hand in it.

Jack was in the same workshop with me, and was quite a
favorite. The convicts often paired off in friendships, and
he and I went together. If either of us had any little
luxury we shared it with the other, as children would do;
and when I got salvation I wanted to share that with him.

I approached him on several occasions with the subject, but he repulsed me with sneers. He seemed to think I was playing a bold game to get out of prison ; but he learned at last that I was in earnest.

He found me several times weeping and poring over my Bible. Once he lifted his hand to strike me, and even spit at me ; but when I told him that I had no resentment, and could stand it for Jesus' sake, he was touched. That astonished him. I said nothing more for a week, and he seemed to be getting worse all the time ; but I felt sure the Spirit of God was striving with him. I kept on praying with strong crying and tears, and I knew God would save him.

One day he told me he had been praying, but it seemed dreadful to him to pray. I knew all about that from my own experience. Not long after this, as he came out of his cell one morning to go to work, I caught sight of his face, and it was all lit up. He was at the head of the column, and I near the foot ; he just glanced at me with a smile, and gave an upward turn of his eye to heaven, and then I knew it was all right with him. I could scarcely keep from shouting.

The first one he told the good news to was the keeper. " Jack," said he, " I'm glad you've got religion." It was not that he cared for religion, but he was afraid of Jack, he was such a desperate character, and now he knew he would have no more trouble with him.

All the time I had to work for Christ was about half an hour each day, and I improved it. This was when the regular keeper was relieved, and we were allowed then to talk. I had my men all picked out, and I went from one to the other, saying the few earnest words I could say.

Several of these were converted. One or two wandered away when they left the prison, having no Christian friend to look after them. Since that time they have come into the Helping Hand, and have been sweetly restored.

About two years I went on thus. My faith was so simple, I felt the Lord would give me anything reasonable I might ask. And I never had a doubt until after I came out of prison and mingled with Christians, and their wavering, unstable, half-and-half faith staggered me. My cell seemed all that time like heaven, and I cared very little whether I ever came out of it or not. The love of Christ was so abounding, it drowned every trouble. No one could insult me. If my comrades abused me, I felt that I could pray for and forgive them.

After this I was led to pray for my liberty. At first I felt that the desire to be set free was of the devil. But I asked the Lord about it, and he gave me the assurance that my desire should be granted. And it was: I received a pardon from the Governor after having served about half my time—seven years and six months.

When I got out of prison I was more lonely than I had been in my cell. I could not go back to my old haunts and companions, and I knew no others. If I had found a single Christian friend at that time, it would have saved me years of misery. And here I must say that it does not seem to me right to turn men out of prison, and make no provision for their future well-doing. Many a poor fellow has been driven to crime, and back again to his prison-cell, for want of kindly counsel and direction when he first came out again into the world.

I wanted to do right, to please God. The first thing I did was to inquire for a prayer-meeting. I was told of one ;

but when I got to the door I was afraid to go in. I had never been to a Protestant meeting, and nobody invited me in. I kept steadily away from the Fourth Ward, lest I should be tempted by old associates. Unfortunately the only friend I found directed me to a lager-bier saloon to board. Lager-bier had come up since I went to prison, and I did not know what it was. They told me it was a harmless drink, wholesome and good, and simple as root-beer. I drank it, and then began my downfall. My head got confused. The old appetite was awakened. From that time I drank it every day, and it was not long before I went from that to stronger liquors.

The night I stopped praying I shall never forget. I felt as wretched as I did the day I went to prison. And now I began a career of sin and misery which I cannot fully describe. Satan got completely the upper hand of me. The dear Saviour who had been so gracious and so precious to me in the prison I let go. How I wonder now that he did not let me go! But he did not.

I had obtained work in a large hat-shop. The workmen had a strike, and I was one of the ringleaders. We were all dismissed, and thus I was thrown out of employment. Then, it being war-time, I went into the bounty business. Rascally business, that. I would pick men up wherever I could find them, get them half drunk, and coax them to enlist. They received the bounty, and I had a premium on each of half the amount. I made a great deal of money in this way, which I spent freely. I became a sporting man, went often to the races, and my downward course was greatly quickened.

I got in with a man, who has since died of delirium tremens, and went boating with him on the river. We would buy stolen goods of the sailors, compel them to enlist on fear of being arrested, and we took the bounty. We went on for some time in this thieving, racing, speculating, and bounty business. We kept a recruiting-office in New York and another in Brooklyn, and found plenty to do, and might have grown rich if I had saved what I made.

But all this time my conscience was far from easy. I remembered the days at Sing-Sing when the glory of the Lord shone in my cell, and I was shouting with joy for sins forgiven, and improving every moment to win souls to Christ. I knew I was all wrong, and yet I could not stop. I seemed to be on a down track, and rushing at furious speed. When I felt the most troubled I would go to drinking, and try to drown conscience in whiskey.

After the war was over I went to boating exclusively, buying and selling smuggled and stolen goods. There was a good deal of this business among sailors and captains. I gave counterfeit money for the goods, until I became well known for this, and then I had to give it up, for no one would steal for me when they found I gave them nothing for it. From this I became a river-thief, boarding vessels at night, and doing the stealing myself. How many narrow escapes from death I had while engaged in this wicked business!

One night we were out on the river in our boat, looking for chances. We had been disappointed in some of our plans at Greenpoint, and pulled down to the Williamsburg ferry, where we fastened our craft to the Idaho, one of the regular ferryboats, to be towed across to the New York side. We had steamed out a little way into the river, when the Idaho was discovered to be on fire. It seemed but the work of a moment from the first alarm, till the whole boat was in flames. The greatest confusion prevailed among the crew and passengers. We let go as soon as we could, for fear we should be swamped; but before we could push off two men jumped in. We rowed them to the shore and then came back, not to save life, but to get booty. Another ferryboat came alongside and rescued about forty of the passengers, but there were ten or twelve who threw themselves into the water, and these we picked up. We saved one Christian woman. We held on to her as she clinched the sides of the boat with her hands. The whole scene was terrific. ' The fire raging, the screams of the perishing, the struggles of the poor creatures in the water, impressed my mind deeply with the thought of the last day and the fiery hell to which I knew the sinner must go. And yet God used us wicked people in the midst of all this terror and confusion to save his children. My partner wanted me to let the people go, and pick up the cloaks, hats, and various things that were floating in the river; but I said, "No; I haven't got so low as that yet." And I thank God now he helped me do what he did, and get all those poor people safe to the land.

Another night in Brooklyn we stole a rope-fender off a ship, the whole value of which was not more than a dollar and a half, and yet for that we could run such fearful risks. The captain of the vessel saw us, and seizing his revolver fired at us, once, twice, four times. The balls came so close that I could feel them as they whizzed past my head, but they did not hit. God preserved me that time also; for what?

After I got round the wharf and out of danger, I felt frightened more than before. Something whispered, "If that bullet had hit you, where would you have been?" and the response of my conscience was, "In hell."

All the time I was prosecuting this business, I had a longing in my sober moments to be a better man, to lead an honest and sober life ; but I felt that after all the joy and peace I had before had, I never could come to God again. Satan always quoted that text to me, " For it is impossible for those who were once enlightened, and have tasted of the heavenly gift, and were made partakers of the Holy Ghost, . . . if they shall fall away, to renew them again unto repentance." So to quell these memories and convictions, I kept all the time under the influence of liquor. If any one had spoken to me kindly and in a Christian spirit at that time, it would have subdued me, but no one came near the poor, wretched outcast.

One night we went over to Brooklyn on a plundering expedition. I was very drunk. There was a certain vessel at the wharf which we had our eye upon, but I was too intoxicated to do my share of the work, so I stayed in the boat while my partner boarded the ship. By some mishap I fell into the water. The boat went one way, and the eddy carried me in another direction, and out from the wharf. I went down and touched bottom, and rose to the surface. Again I sank and rose. The third time, the thought came to me, " This is the last, and now you are gone—you are drowned." Hell seemed opening under my feet, and I fancied I could hear the wails and shrieks of the lost. Then something said, " Call on God." But how could I ? I felt it was too mean ; I had sinned too fearfully. But I did call, and the Lord heard me. I seemed to be lifted right up to the surface of the water, and the boat, which had drifted off in another direction, was brought right to me, so that I could get hold of it. I can't tell how it was, but it always seemed to me a miracle. The water had sobered me, and after I got hold of the boat I managed to get in. After I was in, something seemed to say to me, "God has saved you for the last time. If you ever go out on the river again, God will let you drop into hell and be lost." It was a very clear, strong impression on my mind, but instead of softening me it made me angry.

I took my partner into the boat without a word. We rowed across the river, and I went home and dried my clothes. What a load of guilt was upon me! I could think of nothing else to do, and to rid myself of it I drank, and drank, and drank. But no amount of liquor could drown that inward voice. In spite of all, I would have gone out again, but my partner met with an accident which prevented his going, so, notwithstanding my desires, I did not. We had no money; I couldn't borrow, and I was actually in want.

This may seem strange to some; but while we made a good deal of money in our wicked life, we laid up nothing, but spent as fast as we got it. It was the wages of iniquity, and as the Bible says, " put into a bag with holes," so that it did us no good.

The sting of conscience remained with me, and a strange desire to be out of this wicked business, and in some honorable employment. It seemed wonderful that such feelings should so haunt me all the time ; but now I can see that it was the convicting power of the Holy Spirit that was pursuing me, and would not let me go until I had been brought back from my wanderings.

The John Allen excitement had just commenced in Water Street, and the good Christian people were going through the ward to bring in the sinners to the meetings. I was sitting in my room one of these wretched days, when I heard

a stranger in the hall below. The landlady was ill up-stairs,
and the person who had entered came up. Just outside my
door I heard a pleasant voice say to her, "Do you love
Jesus?" That voice—those words! It seemed like long-
forgotten music. It recalled the past happy days when I
had known the love of Jesus, and my heart was deeply
touched.

" No, indade, do I love Jesus; and who is he?" was the
rough answer I heard.

" My good woman, and don't you know who Jesus is?"
and then the person passed on to the top of the house, to
see another inmate of the house, whom he had been sent to
visit, and the landlady came into my room.

" Who is that?" said I.

" Oh, it's one of them tract pedlers," said she.

" Why don't you treat the man with respect?" said I.

She was silent, but I thought at once that perhaps this
man, whoever he might be, might get me a job of honest
work; so I went out and waited on the landing till he came
down-stairs. He saw me; but I was a frightful-looking object, and I think he was a little scared at facing me. However, I accosted him, and he told me to come down-stairs
and he would talk with me. I had a colored shirt on, an
old pair of pants, and my hair was cropped pretty close. I
don't wonder the missionary didn't want to talk with me on
the landing, but preferred to have me below on the pave-
ment.

We walked out together, up the street, till we came to
the New Bowery. As we approached the Howard Mission
he invited me in. I didn't know until then that there was
such a place. A gentleman there met us, and spoke to me
very kindly. They both said that if I would sign the pledge

they would see what they could do for me. The idea struck me as it never had done before, that a drunkard like me couldn't get work, and there was no hope of decent employment unless I did reform. So I signed it. But I told them I shouldn't be likely to keep it, that I had taken it many times before, and broken it. I wanted to be honest, but I knew I couldn't keep it. "Try it again," they both said, "and ask God to help you." "Well, to please you, I will," I said.

I went right home from there and told my partner what I had done. How he laughed! "You take the pledge!" he said. He had a bottle of gin in his hand at that moment, and turning out a glass offered it to me. "Tom," said I, "I have just taken the pledge." But I drank it; and as I put down the glass, I added, "Now this is the last drink I shall ever take." "Yes, till you get the next," said he.

Just at that moment in walked the missionary. I kept as far away from him as I could, so that he might not smell my breath. I think if he had asked me I should have honestly confessed what I had done. But he did not. He only invited me to go out and walk with him. I went; and as we walked I told him I was going out on the river that night, for we were dead broke, I was hungry, and must have money.

He looked sad and troubled. "Jerry," said he, "before you shall do that, I'll take this coat off my back and pawn it, and give you the money."

I looked at the coat and saw it was worn and old, and I was touched to the heart. It was as much as I could do to keep the tears out of my eyes. "Here's this good man," I said to myself, "poor, as I know he must be, willing to take the coat off his back and pawn it to keep me from doing wrong." I don't know as he saw the effect of his words, but I hung my head.

"I will give you a text out of the Bible," said he. "'Seek ye first the kingdom of God, and his righteousness, and all these things shall be added unto you.'"

I remember my answer: "I'll take that text and trust God."

Then he went away, and in a little while he brought me fifty cents. I got something to eat, and we did not go out boating.

The next day, as Tom and I, with Maria (now my beloved wife and helper) and Nellie, the two girls with whom Tom and I were intimate, were in our room together, the missionary with some Christian ladies came in to see us. They talked with us a while, and then said they would pray. I wished they wouldn't, but I had not the courage to say so, and they went on. Those prayers had a wonderful effect upon me.

Day after day my new friend followed me up, and so closely that I could get no chance to drink. "Tom," I would say, "I'm going to turn over a new leaf." But Tom would answer, "Will the Lord come down from heaven to give you a beefsteak?" The missionary would often repeat the text he had given me, but Tom wouldn't accept it. I felt, however, that I could. I had had some experience which he had not, and I believed the Word of the Lord.

Soon after this we were invited to the missionary's house to take tea. He lent me a coat to wear. After tea they had singing and prayer. I cried and cried.

"Pray for yourself," said he, "and God will save you."

"I don't know how," I said; "I can't put the words to-gether." It wasn't that I had forgotten all about praying; but after I had sinned so fearfully, I felt afraid to utter such solemn words.

"Pray the prayer of the publican," some one cried; "'God be merciful to me a sinner.'"

I prayed it. My heart was all broken, and I repeated the words over and over.

"Put in 'For Jesus' sake,'" said the missionary.

So I put that in, and .oh, the joy that came into my heart: not like the first time, but more calm and peaceful.

"I am saved," I cried; "Jesus has saved me."

Oh, the joy and excitement of that evening! I shall never forget it. These good people had come down into the Fourth Ward to labor among the very lowest of low and wicked men and women, and God had given them a trophy in me, one of the hardest cases in the ward. How their faith was strengthened!

After that the missionary used often to walk round with me, his arm in mine. This was a great help to me, for all my old companions had heard of my conversion, and it was such a strange event that they would shout after me. So it was a protection to be with some one whom they truly respected. It is not so much of an event now for a notorious sinner to be converted in Water Street. The wonders of God's grace have been greatly multiplied down there within the last few years.

But before this came about I had a long and trying probation. I found work in the Ferry Company. There I was tempted, and drank again. My good friend the missionary had left the city, the meetings were given up, and I felt lonely and sad. I had not then joined any church.

Maria was out of the city, and I felt I must go and see her. I took Sunday for the visit, though conscience told me I was doing wrong. It was a cold, snowy day. I went in the stage, and when we reached the half-way house all the passengers got out and drank. They looked at me as they were taking their hot whiskey, seemingly with pity, as though I couldn't afford to buy. My pride was touched. I went up to the bar and asked for sarsaparilla. The man handed me a gin-bottle and glass. There was an inward conflict, and I grieved the Spirit.

Coming back from my visit, I lost the stage, and had to put in at a hotel. There the devil made me drink again. I could only think of the house " empty, swept and garnished," where the unclean spirit had dwelt. " Then goeth he, and taketh with himself seven other spirits more wicked than himself, and they enter in and dwell there; and the last state of that man is worse than the first." The unclean spirit had come back into my heart with his miserable company, and I was in a sad plight.

I went out of the hotel and went straight to a church which was open. I sat down, and though I was drunk, I seemed to know what was going on. I was very angry with myself, and cursed God. I said, " I'll never go back to Water Street, to disgrace God and the good people there." I made up my mind I would kill myself.

I went out from the church and took the cars for home. What a day I had spent! My brain was on fire. My heart was cast down. My conscience was sore. Yes, I thought again, " I will kill myself." I made up my mind to let my-self down from the platform and let the cars go over me.

But the conductor was there and pushed me in. While I was watching my opportunity the Holy Spirit came to me, and my heart was softened. The next night I went to a meeting, confessed my sin, and asked Christians to pray for me, and I prayed myself that God would forgive me.

I fell once after that, but God lifted me up again.

The Sunday after this last slip I went into the Howard Mission, while the Sunday-school children were singing. I sat down on a side seat, and then I saw on the platform the gentleman mentioned in the next chapter who had previously been introduced to me by the missionary, and had spoken kind and encouraging words to me. He looked at me and recognized me with a friendly smile and nod. I felt ashamed to look him in the face. Just before the meeting closed I got up and slipped out of the door for fear he would come and speak to me. I did not want him to know that I had been going wrong. But he was too quick for me. He caught me in the passage outside the chapel-door before I could get down the steps. He held out his hand, and, seeing my downcast looks, said, " What is the matter, Jerry?" I held back my hand and said, " I am not fit for you to speak to me." He said "Why, what is the trouble ; tell me all about it?" I then said " I have been in hell for three days," and I told him what had happened. He gave me a warm squeeze of the hand, and then, putting both his hands on my shoulders and looking me straight in the eye, with his own moist with sympathy, he said, " Don't give it up, Jerry; try again, and keep trying, and hold on to Jesus." His words and look and hearty grip strengthened and encouraged me wonderfully.

All this time I had kept up the use of tobacco, and that created a thirst in me. And I didn't belong to any church,

and so had no Christian influence to hold me. But soon
after that I joined a Methodist Church on probation, and
that strengthened me.

I had another trial. I was required to work on Sunday.
I told my employer I was not only reformed, but trying to
lead a Christian life.

"Jerry," said he, "you are no better than I. I am a
Christian man, but I have to work on Sunday, and you
must too. I want you to come to-morrow to work."

But I felt it was wrong, and did not go. On Monday
morning I was discharged. I felt badly, for he was a
church-member, and I a poor weak beginner in the Christian life.

"Never mind," said my boss, trying to console me;
"you go to work and I guess it will be all right."

"No, I won't," said I; "I will trust God."

But I would not leave until I had seen my employer. I
found him leaning over the side of the ferryboat. I tapped
him on the shoulder.

"Captain C.," said I, "have you discharged me for wishing to keep the Sabbath?"

He made no answer, but I knew he had heard me. I
tapped him on the shoulder again.

"Captain C., have you discharged me for trying to do
right?"

"Jerry," said he, "you haven't accommodated me, and I
can't accommodate you."

"Good-morning," said I, and walked away.

After I began to try to live right, I went on for some
time without work; then my friend the missionary came
back, and introduced me to Mr. H., a rich gentleman in the
city. Mr. H. shook hands with me, and told me to keep

on doing right, to trust God, and when I was in want to
come down to his office and see him; and he gave me his
number. The shake of his hand and his encouraging words
built me up. I resolved that I would never go to him for
money, but his kindness put new life into me; and I often
went to him after that for encouragement and advice. No
matter how busy he was, he always had a kind word for
me, and would often excuse himself from his big friends to
talk with me.

CHAPTER III.

JERRY BECOMES A MISSIONARY.

" Chosen, not for good in me,
  Wakened up from wrath to flee,
  Hidden in the Saviour's side
  By thy Spirit sanctified;
  Teach me here on earth to show
  By my love, how much I owe!"

SOON after this I got a job of work, was led into scenes of
temptation, and fell again.   But this was the last time.   I
resolved to give up tobacco, went into a Christian family
who found employment for me, and I gave myself wholly
to God.

And here let me say a word about tobacco.   I consider it
a great stumbling-block in any Christian's life ; but when a
man has had an appetite for liquor and is trying to keep
from drinking, the use of tobacco is positively fatal.   It will
surely bring him back to his cups.   If I had given it up
when I gave up rum, I believe I should have had none of
those fearful falls which I have described.   I was led at last,
by the grace of God, to do the clean thing—to give up
every sinful habit, and from that time Jesus has kept me.

After a time my work ceased, but the money I had saved
lasted me some time.   When I got to the last five dollars,
I went into my room and prayed most earnestly for work,
and before I came out I felt the assurance that my prayer

was answered. In a few days a situation was offered me in the custom-house for four dollars a day. But there I preached Jesus too much, and was soon turned away.

Then I got steady employment in another place, where also I testified for Jesus. I had been there only a little while before a companion began to swear. I reproved him.

" We can get along without swearing," said I.

" What !" said he, " are you a churchman ?"

" No, I am a Christian, or trying to be one," I replied.

So I was spotted among the workmen, and pointed out as one of the " hypocrites." One man, a German, I was permitted to lead to Christ.

One day I had a sort of trance or vision. I was singing at my work, and my mind became absorbed, and it seemed as if I was working for the Lord down in the Fourth Ward. I had a house, and people were coming in. There was a bath, and as they came in I washed and cleansed them outside, and the Lord cleansed them inside. They came at the first by small numbers, then by hundreds, and afterwards by thousands.

Before I came out of this vision I was in tears. Then something said to me, " Would you do that for the Lord if he should call you? Would you do it for Jesus' sake?" And I answered, " Yes, Lord, open the way, and I will go." I felt that I could go down there where I had always lived. I was used to the filth and misery, the drunkenness and Romanism, and I wasn't afraid of them. I felt sure I should be called to work for Jesus down there.

A little while after that my health gave way, and I took a vacation. I went with my wife to Sea Cliff, to attend the camp-meeting. All the time the thought of this work was

pressing upon me, and I prayed God to open the way for
me to talk to the Christian people there about it.   He gave
me the opportunity.   From there I went to Sing-Sing
camp-ground, and presented it, and afterwards to Ocean
Grove.   Many were interested in the proposed work, and
gave me larger or smaller sums to help it along, until I held
in trust four hundred and fifty dollars.

Then the Lord opened the way for me to begin the work
in a small way at 316 Water Street, next door to where
John Allen's dance-house used to be, and where the meetings had been held in which I had first testified for Jesus
after I had been brought back to him in the way I have re-
lated.   The house had previously been a notorious dance-
house of the worst sort.   At the time of the John Allen excitement as it was called, of which I have already spoken,
the lease of the house had been bought by my friend Mr.
H. ; the dance-house people had been turned out with all
their ungodly traps, and the building opened for a mission.   Afterwards when the lease had run out and the
owner wouldn't renew it, Mr. H. bought the property so
that it might be kept for a mission.   There were a good
many around there who would have been glad to see it
turned into a devil's mission again ; but they were disappointed.

At the time when the Lord put it into my heart to begin
a mission, the house was occupied as a kind of side-station
by the City Mission and Tract Society, to whom Mr. H. had
given the use of it.

I went to him one Sunday at the Howard Mission and
told him about what I wanted to do, and about the four
hundred and fifty dollars that I had raised.   He seemed to
discourage me a little at first.   He said, " Jerry, if you start a

mission you will have to give your time to it ; you have got a good situation and good wages, where you are respected and trusted, which you will have to give up. Don't you think you can serve God and do good and earn your bread and butter at the same time right where you are?" I thought then, and I knew afterwards, that he was trying me to see how much I was in earnest. I told him my heart was set on working for the salvation of such as I used to be ; that I was sure the Lord had put me up to it, and that I was willing to trust Him. He looked at me a minute, and then, putting his hand on my shoulder, and smiling as if convinced, he said, " Well, Jerry, there is the old house in Water Street ; it belongs to me ; you may have the use of that. I will speak to the City Mission people and get them to give it up ; go ahead, and God bless you. I will help you all I can."

The City Mission and Tract Society, at his suggestion, cheerfully consented to leave the house at our disposal. We went down there in October, 1872, laid out the four hundred and fifty dollars in cleaning and repairing the house, and opened the place as a resort for the forlorn way-farers, sailors, and others who frequented the locality. We put up a sign, " Helping Hand for Men," which has been the guide-board to bring many a poor soul to the foot of the cross.

No one need suppose that I could undertake and go on in such a work without opposition. My relatives, and my wife's also, were Roman Catholics, and were greatly dis-pleased with us. One of my sisters came to talk with me. I tried to convince her of the truth from the Scriptures. I told her there was no other name given under heaven whereby men can be saved but the name of Jesus. I could

not convince her, nor she me, so she went to one of the
priests about it.

"I am a cònverted Protestant," said he, "and know both
sides, and I will soon fix him."

My sister wanted me to go with her to see him. I had
no desire to go for the sake of argument, but for her sake
I said I would, to show her too that I was not afraid. She
couldn't read, and didn't believe what I had told her of the
Bible. "But," said I, "the priest is a learned man, and he
will know that I speak the truth." My wife went with us,
and a niece who had been brought up in a convent, and was
very bigoted and bitter against the Protestants.

"You have come here to be convinced of your errors,"
said the priest, as we seated ourselves in his room.

"I did," said I, "if you can convince me from the Bible.
Excuse me one moment, father; do you believe it to be an
inspired book?"

"Certainly."

"Do you believe this of the Protestant Bible?"

"Certainly; there is but little difference."

"I am glad you feel so, to start with," I said.

"You will allow the Catholic Church to be the first," he
said to me.

"Yes, if you leave the Roman out," I answered. But he
took no notice of that.

"Christ said," he went on, "that the gates of hell should
not prevail against his Church. Now if the gates of hell
have prevailed, Christ was a liar."

That sounded hard, and I felt that my Master was in-
sulted, but I kept quiet.

"I want to show you," he said, "that the gates of hell
have not prevailed. The first Church was made up of the

twelve apostles. One of these was a traitor; but the gates didn't prevail then, and haven't since. Have you ever read the history of Rome? Well, they were fearfully wicked in Luther's time. They themselves acknowledged that the Church was corrupt and needed reformation. But still the Church did not go down. Do you believe Luther was a good man? He could not have been, for no man is good who breaks his vows."

"A bad vow is better broken than kept," I said; but he did not reply to that.

"Do you believe in the Mass?" he asked.

"No, I never read of the Mass or Confession in the Bible. It is a most degrading thing to bow down before a fellow-man to worship him."

"You are not required to do that. We take the sins on us, and stand between you and God."

"Then you stand in the place of Christ. Now God says, 'Go into your closet, and pray in secret, and he will reward openly.' Isn't prayer the same thing with confession?"

He owned that it was, but said, "Does not James say, 'Confess your faults one to another'?"

"Yes," said I, "that is just what we do in our prayer-meetings. When we have been led into sin we say so, and repent and come to Jesus, and testify of his willingness to receive us."

"Well, that's right."

"And now," said I, "while we are on this point, you have as good a right to confess to me as I have to confess to you. 'Confess to one another,' the Bible says. Then what do you do with these verses: 'There is none other name given under heaven among men whereby we can be saved,' and, 'There is one mediator between God and man, the man Christ Jesus'? You presume to be the mediator. You take my sister's sins, for instance, on yourself, you say, and bear them to God."

Then I told him my experience. " I have been a drunkard and a thief, one of the wickedest men that ever lived. I have been in State prison, and yet this Jesus, who is despised in your Church, has picked me up out of the gutter, has washed and cleansed and saved me. But you say all the Protestants will be damned."

"Oh, no," said he, "no; I believe that every good Protestant will go to heaven; but the turn-coats—they will surely be lost."

" My sister can tell you what a bad man I was, and what has been done for me. According to your theory, this is just to fit me for hell, and it must be the work of Satan."

" Satan often becomes an angel of light."

"Then he certainly has become a friend to me. But no, that is not so; I am not a slave of Satan, I am a free man. Jesus has set me free, as the Bible says he will do for every one that believes in him."

" We don't follow the Bible."

" What do you follow ?"

" The traditions of the Church."

" I didn't come here to argue, Father G., but to convince my sister of the truth. I am not afraid of the priest. The Lord has opened my eyes. Your people are afraid of you. You will lie to benefit the Church; but God has said, 'All liars shall have their part in the lake that burneth with fire and brimstone.'"

I talked fearlessly and faithfully to him. My heart was full of peace and joy, and I believe the Lord that night ful-

Mrs. MARIA McAULEY.

filled his word, and made the weak and foolish things to confound the wise.

I feel that a word about my wife, and the way in which she was led to Christ, will be appropriate here. She too was the fruit of Water Street mission-work, and I am sure that my work at the Helping Hand would not be half so successful as it is without her. She is truly a helpmeet from the Lord to me.

She was, like myself, a Romanist, brought up in superstition and bigotry. When she grew up she was obliged, like thousands of others, to earn her own living, and for that purpose came to the city. Here she was exposed to temptation on every side. She went into worldly pleasures, as young people are apt to do, and before long acquired a love for drink. About the time of my conversion she was invited into the John Allen Mission. She attended the meetings, but the gospel invitations she heard did not seem to do her any good. They fell upon her ear, but that was all. They sounded to her, as she often says, like an unknown tongue. And yet they were not altogether new, for they called up to her memory things she had heard in her childhood, when she had been a member of a Protestant Sunday-school. And here, I think, is encouragement for Christian people to bring in such children into their Mission Sunday-schools, even if they do belong to another faith.

The mission-workers labored with Maria very kindly and faithfully, but still she was not converted. She did, however, promise to give up drinking, and after a while was persuaded to leave the city, and to take a situation in a Christian family in the country. Her friends hoped that in this way, by leaving the places of temptation, and living among good people, she would be brought to choose the right way.

Here she was taught in religious things, attended family worship, and read the Bible, but still her heart was not reached.

After several months she left this home for another. This too was a Christian family, and she had the same privileges, and here it was that suddenly the truths of the gospel were revealed to her. They came to her, just as knowledge seems to open to a little child, we don't know how, only we find, when we are not looking for it, that the child knows. Her blind eyes in an unexpected moment were touched, and she saw; her deaf ears were unstopped, and she heard. The way of salvation opened before her, and the words she had so often heard, and which had slipped off from her like water from a rock, were all at once full of life and power. They took hold of her conscience and heart; the lessons of her childhood came to her with a meaning they had never had, and she believed on the Lord Jesus Christ, and was saved.

When Jesus was revealed to her she received him gladly, and gave herself wholly to him. It was no half-way work with her. Her faith was childlike, her love simple and earnest. She at once received power to lift her out of the bondage of sinful appetite, and her soul was possessed with a love for sinners, and a desire to lead others to the same precious Saviour she had found. She could not rest day or night for the longing she had to tell the glad story of her salvation.

She came back to the city and commenced missionary work, in the employ of some Christian ladies, as a Bible-reader in the Fourth Ward. She found easy access to tenement-houses, liquor-saloons, and dens of infamy, and in every place testified of the grace of Christ, and besought sinners to behold the Lamb of God, who taketh away the sins of the world. Many listened, forsook their evil ways, and came to Jesus, who are living witnesses for the Lord to-day.

I bless God that He permitted us to be united, and to work together in the Helping Hand; and I hope God will let us live a great while to labor for souls. We find it sweet to work for him, and though we know we are in ourselves very weak and helpless, and prone to mistakes, yet we trust in the Lord, and feel that his precious blood is applied every moment to cleanse and save us. Glory be to Jesus!

By the kindness of some Christian friends in the city, a dinner was provided on Thanksgiving Day, soon after we took possession of the Mission-house. Bountiful provision was made, and the needy and outcast were freely invited to come in. The day closed with a religious service, and the Holy Spirit was poured upon the assembled company. It was a time long to be remembered; and under its solemn influence the Lord put it into our hearts to appoint a similar meeting for the next evening. From that time to the present, now more than three years, the humble chapel of the Helping Hand has been opened and lighted every evening for a gospel service. Hundreds of souls have been converted to God in this hallowed spot. The Lord has truly honored the place and the work.

The meetings are led by Christians of various denominations in New York and Brooklyn, and it is wonderful how the workers have been blest of God in their earnest effort to do good to others. I am on the spot all the time with my wife, and our work is by no means confined to the evening service. Multitudes of poor sinful ones come in during the day for help and counsel. We point them to Jesus, the great Physician and Helper of body and soul, and many a one has it been our pleasure to lead to the fountain opened for sin and uncleanness.

But my vision is not yet fully realized. The house of the Lord, with the bath, the chapel, and all the furnishings which I saw, has not yet been given. It is the dearest hope of my life to see it. I pray daily that the Lord will provide the means to put up just such a building, for it is needed in this Fourth Ward, as a refuge and safe harbor for the poor souls tossed up and down on the billows of sin and misery. And I have faith to believe that in God's own good time it will be accomplished.*

Meanwhile we are watching for souls, humbly trusting in the grace of God and the gift of his Holy Spirit, which alone can draw them out of the bondage of Satan into the liberty of children of God.

This short sketch of my life I now lay as an offering on God's altar. I have told enough of my sin to magnify the riches of divine grace which reached out the hand of love and gently drew me in from the depths of iniquity into his loving favor. My prayer is, that the story of what Jesus

---

* In the year 1876 the old building at 316 Water Street in which Jerry commenced his work was torn down, and a substantial three-story brick building was erected for the use of the Mission on the same spot; thus realizing in great measure his vision, and the hopes and aspirations to which it had given birth. About this time the Mission was incorporated under the title of *The McAuley Water Street Mission*, and became the owner of the property free from debt. Its work still goes on, constantly illustrating the power of Jesus to save, perpetuating the memory of its founder, and honoring the Redeemer whom he loved and served.

has done for me may encourage other sinners to trust in him for the same glorious, free salvation.

NOTE.—We have now come to the end of the little work "Transformed," published by Jerry. He intended writing a larger volume during the winter of 1884-85, and would no doubt have done so had not death ended his earthly labors. Happily some further accounts of his work were dictated by Jerry from time to time before his death and these have furnished the material for many of the succeeding pages.

CHAPTER IV.

TRIALS AND TRIUMPHS.

"When we cannot see our way,
We should trust and still obey;
He who bids us forward go,
Will instruct the way to know."

In the preceding chapter brief reference was made to the origin of the Water Street Mission meetings. Speaking later to a friend of the Thanksgiving there mentioned, Jerry thus described the memorable occasion:

"On Thanksgiving we gave a good dinner to one hundred and fifty poor people; and afterwards we had a kind of a family prayer-meeting, Brother Rue proposing to give thanks for the grand day we had experienced. We got together for prayer and singing, and while this was going on the outside people flocked in and crowded the house.

"Such a sight I never saw: sinners crying, 'God have mercy on me!' 'Lord help me!' and while I was on my knees the Lord said, 'You had better open the door every evening.' And so I did; and this was the beginning of the grand revival since carried on at the Water Street Mission, commencing in such a humble way, and yet doing such a great work among all sorts of people—rich and poor, high and low."

All along the work was one of faith. Feeding many needy persons every day, even with the simple food provided, and carrying on the meetings every night, was not accomplished without means. But Jerry believed that the work was God's, and that so long as God wished him to carry it on the money would be forthcoming.

So the testing times were trusting times, and days of trial were days of happy triumph; for God greatly honored the humble faith of these two earnest ones. Jerry says:

"As we had made it a rule to neither beg nor run in debt, our finances would frequently run very low, and we found ourselves more than once with very little in the treasury; then again we would feel rich when we found we had $10 in cash. We borrowed no trouble about finances, but trusted wholly in the Lord."

In the first printed report we find many incidents serving to illustrate the spirit in which the work was carried on. From among these we select the two following:

"Before the cold weather set in the workers prayed earnestly for the winter's supply of coal. Two business men were talking about it just then in their office downtown. One of these men had been converted but a few months before at the Mission, and felt moved to send in a thank-offering to the Lord. The other had been for many months a devoted worker there. Said the first, 'Let us join and send them coal enough to last the winter months.' The thought was of God, before whom the earnest prayer had just gone up. It was done, and all trouble on that score was settled.

"On another occasion a gas-bill came in, and there was not a cent in the treasury; but it was taken to the Father, to whom belongs the silver and the gold. In the course of the day a letter was received containing just the amount of the bill, and the car-fare of the messenger who should go to pay it."

4

During the first year of this useful work 26,261 meals were furnished to hungry men, lodgings were given to 5144, and a great deal of clothing was supplied. This was all done without any accumulation of debt, money coming to hand as it was needed.

Of two instances in which his faith was tried, but was found firm and proved victorious, Jerry thus speaks:

" I call to mind one instance, and relate it to show how we were led. One night we found the Mission without a cent, and forty odd tramps to feed and nothing to offer them. It was a time to test my views, for I had declared I would let the Lord have his way, and whenever he ceased to provide, I would accept it as an evidence that he did not want us to go on, and as he supplied our necessities, would consider he was pleased to have us continue. I felt for those poor hungry men. Some of them had probably not tasted a bit of food for two and three days; they had no money to help themselves, and when they came on Saturday night we usually kept them over Sunday, but on this night we were broke.

" We proceeded to the Mission-room and commenced the services, and some souls were saved. But even when nine o'clock had come, strange to say no one had handed us a penny. As the meeting drew to a close and nothing came, oh how dark everything looked; my faith trembled. I could hardly keep from crying as I looked into the hungry faces of my poor tramps and converts. I spoke to my wife about them, and she replied:

" ' The Lord will provide; you see if he don't ! '

" I closed with a heavy heart and dismissed the meeting, and my wife took her position at the door, as usual, to shake hands with the folks as they went out. A lady passed out with her husband, and after going five or ten yards suddenly stopped, and coming back to my wife said, ' Mrs. McAuley, we keep a baker-shop in Cherry Street, and I just happened to think you had better send up and get $5 worth of bread ! '   There was God's hand in answer to prayer, and we soon had enough for all and some to spare.

"Another time we had used our last cent.   We said nothing about it in the meeting, but prayed secretly for the dear Lord to interpose for us.   Meeting was dismissed, and shortly after the people began to leave a man came in from the street and handed me a package.   I opened it, and to my astonishment found $100 in it.   The sight of it nearly took my breath away.   I looked at it a moment, and then at the poor fellow who brought it, and finally said to him, ' Where in the world did you get this? '   ' A man gave it to me just outside, and told me to hand it to you,' he replied. ' Who was he? ' I said, as I turned it over and looked at it on every side to see if there wasn't something wrong about it. ' I don't know,' said the man, who now seemed as much surprised as I was.   ' A man out on the sidewalk handed it to me, and said, " Here, hand that to Jerry ;" that's all I know.' I counted it again : it was all there—one hundred dollars ! ' Whew ! ' said I, we'll never be poor again ! '

"Thus the Lord always interfered, but generally not until we were actually or pretty nearly dead broke and really needed it, proving himself a ' present help in time of trouble.' "

The financial difficulties of the work were by no means the only ones to be surmounted.

Jerry says, "When the every-night meetings commenced, then also began our troubles, for the devil woke up.   Crowds

of the lowest people used to come to the door to disturb the
meetings, throwing brickbats and garbage, and anything they
could lay their hands on, into the room. The police gave
us no protection at that time, although I saw the captain
time and again, but to no purpose."

It is greatly to be regretted that Jerry should have had
to make such a statement in reference to those who are
paid and pledged to preserve order and keep the low and
vicious under restraint. We would gladly suppress that
part of this record which relates to the police and their ne-
glect of duty, but to do so would be to keep out of sight
some of the severest obstacles with which our brother had
to contend. It is only fair to say, however, that at times
during the history of the work the officials of the particular precinct in which Jerry labored, as well as those at
head-quarters, appreciated him and the work he was doing,
and showed an earnest desire to afford all the protection in
their power. We shall give in Jerry's own words some of
this side of the history of the Water Street work. Those
who knew him best will know that he did not relate such
incidents in a spirit of boastfulness, or to show his own
prowess. They were drawn from him as illustrating the
nature of some of the difficulties which he had to encounter.

" During the early history of the Mission there were two
notorious dens directly opposite our place, on the other
side of the street. These were inhabited by a rabble of the
lowest order, and they used to gather together and yell and
make all sorts of unearthly noises to disturb the meetings.
We found out one day to our great satisfaction that some
wealthy men had purchased the property where these dens
stood, and that they were to be torn down and two new
houses built in their places. We congratulated ourselves

that this was a good thing for us, and a cause for thanks-giving. How little we knew what trouble it was to bring us into, even before the houses were built! Many of the workmen employed on them were a hard lot of drinking, boisterous fellows. Every one that passed along the street was at their mercy, and their language was filthy and brutal beyond all description.

"A young, well-dressed man was passing one day, and one of them turned the hose on him and flooded him with water. Of course he resented the insult, and hard words began to fly back and forth. A crowd soon gathered, and after considerable talk the laborer threatened to knock out the young fellow's brains with a pickaxe, and the latter dared him to do it. I was standing in the door of the Mission looking quietly on, when, as the workman raised himself, as likely as not to split the young man's head open, his eye caught sight of me. Whether he thought I was in the way of his taking vengeance on the stranger, or whether he was loaded up with bitterness on account of what he had heard about the Mission, I do not know, but in a moment he turned all his venom upon me. 'What are you looking at, you dirty turncoat, you miserable hypocrite, you?' he yelled, and followed with a torrent of foul words. I was astonished, and said to him, 'See here, you must remember we are not all of us bad here, and if you don't shut up that foul mouth of yours, I'll take you to the station-house.' 'Come over here, you,' he yelled in fury, adding a lot more of his vile words. Then I walked over and caught hold of him by the collar. I had a deputy-sheriff's badge, and had the right to make arrests. As I grabbed him his 'pal' slipped up behind me, and swing-ing his great heavy shovel over his shoulder, was about to hit me. But I gave the fellow I had hold of a shove, and landed him into a great pile of loose sand brought there for building purposes, and while he was scrambling and floundering to get out I piled the other fellow on top of him. It was enough to make any one laugh to see those fellows trying to get out of the soft sand, and afraid all the time I was going for them again. Seeing a policeman coming I beckoned to him, and ordered him to arrest the scoundrel who began the row. He was about to do so when another policeman came running up. He took in the situation, and whispered something in the first one's ear. It was only a word, but it acted like magic. The M. P dropped his prisoner, and without a word grabbed me by the collar and arrested me as the offender. Of course I made no objection to going with him, although I knew he had no business to arrest a man wearing a badge and in the performance of his duty.

" How delighted the rabble were ; and the policemen, entering into their spirit, gave them a good chance to gloat over their seeming victory, by walking me as slowly as possible down that wicked street to show me up. ' There he goes,' yelled one. ' See the dirty turncoat !' ' Bad luck to the likes of ye !' screamed another, and so on, with oaths, curses, and blasphemies, devoting me to any place but heaven, and wishing me anything but blessings. We reached the station-house, and the joy of the officials over catching such a troublesome fish was plain enough.

" One of the workmen made the complaint that I struck the other on the nose and knocked him down. ' Is that so ? ' said the sergeant ; ' did he hit you ?—show me the marks.' ' Him lave any marks on me ! I'd knock his brains out,' was the reply. ' Arrah, go lang wid ye ! Faith he

did,' insisted the complainant; and they were near coming
to blows between themselves, and made the place ring with
their oaths and hard words. They contradicted each other
so that the officials began to look blue as the hopes of
making out a case against me died away. The foreman of
the building now interfered and said, 'I saw the whole
thing. My men have been drinking a little too much;'
and then he described the affair as it was, concluding by
saying, 'I didn't see him strike either of them.' With
this the captain boiled over as he saw I was going to slip
through his fingers after all, and shaking his fist under my
nose he called me all manner of names, and said, 'I'll lock
you up, anyway. I'll break up that old nuisance of a Mission for you. It keeps the whole place in an uproar. I'll
send you back to prison again, where you belong. That old
Mission is a nuisance.'

"'He has a shield on too, captain,' interrupted the policeman; 'just look at him! and he has a great big club down
there at his ould mission to knock men down wid.' At this
the captain grabbed me by the collar and tore my vest
open, exclaiming, 'I'll take it off you!' I pushed him
back, and raising my finger said, 'Captain, I dare you to
put your finger on that shield!' As I spoke he started for
me again, but the opening of the outside door caught his
attention, and there was my wife coming in. He did not
know her, and growled,

"'What can I do for you, madam?'

"'What are you going to do with that man?' she
questioned.

"'What in —— is that to *you*?' he retorted fiercely.

"'A great deal, sir! He is my husband!' she answered
calmly; and I then interrupted them by saying to her,

'You go see Mr. Dodge or Mr. Hatch.' She hurried down to Mr. A. S. Hatch, who was one of our reliable stand-bys in time of trouble, and told him the story. Mr. Hatch was unable to leave his office just then, but he put her in a carriage and sent her to the Superintendent of the City Missions, with a note. He went with her to Mr. William E. Dodge, Sr., and this noble man of God was all stirred up in a moment. 'Jerry shall not sleep in that place one night if it costs $50,000 to get him out,' he exclaimed. 'Not even if a special court has to be called *immediately !* '

" My wife knew whose hands the case was in, and, as it was now after the time for meeting to commence, she hurried back to the Mission to look after things there. Her heart was sad and heavy as she thought of me up in that old station-house among those lions, and though she had committed me to God, she could not help feeling anxious, and somewhat cast down. In this mood she came to the door of the Mission, and looking inside she started back all in a heap. She has often since spoken of the peculiar feeling she had when, looking into the chapel, she saw the meeting running in good style, and Mr. Jerry McAuley—if you please—sitting in his usual place, leading the meeting. She could hardly believe her eyes, and giving them a good rub took another look and finally concluded that it was either her husband that she had left a short time ago in the hands of the sharks, or his ghost sitting there, or else that the whole thing had been an ugly dream from the beginning. She knew she was wide awake, and as I didn't look very ghostly, she settled the matter quite readily in her own mind, and walked in with a hearty ' Thank God?' and took part in the meeting.

" This was the way I came to be released : The foreman's

statements were hard to reconcile with what the drunken men had said, and what the officials would have been glad enough to prove against me; and so after talking and planning and scratching their heads over it, the sergeant whispered to the others, ' It won't do; that commitment won't stand, so we'd better tear it up;' and suiting the action to the words, he demolished it and scattered it on the floor. The foreman now interposed for his men, and said,

" ' My men have been drinking some, sir; but if you will let us get back to work now I'd like it.' ' Go on,' replied the captain; and then, glaring at me like a wild beast cheated out of a good haul, he said fiercely, ' Get out of here! Get out!'

" ' I thought you were going to lock me up, captain?' I said quietly.

" ' G-e-t o-u-t!' he yelled.

" ' I thought you were going to lock me up?' I continued. ' Now I dare you to do it! Why don't you?'

" ' G-e-t o-u-t!'

" ' Yes, I'll get out,' I replied; ' but mark you, captain, I'll be in this ward when you are turned out of it.' And I was; for shortly after this we heard that he was censured and fined, and he then resigned. But he caused me a great deal of trouble before my prophecy came true; for as soon as I got out of his clutches that time he picked out the very worst man he had on the force—a brutal and foul-mouthed fellow by the name of Fitch—and sent this ' guardian ' as my ' protector,' with orders from headquarters to keep him for just that post. ' Arrah, Jerry,' he said when he came on, '*I'll* make it *hot* for yer!'—and he kept his word."

CHAPTER V.

WATER STREET AS IT WAS.

"Go labor on, spend and be spent,
    Thy joy to do the Father's will;
It was the way the Master went,
    Shall not the servant tread it still?"

But even Fitch was more than matched by Savage, another officer whose beat included the street in front of the Mission-house. An account of some of this man's proceedings we find prefaced with a reference to Jerry's campaign against the dens by which he was surrounded. The terrible condition of the neighborhood in which the Mission was located is only too vividly seen by this account.

Jerry says: "About this time I became so grieved over the desolation and wickedness all around us that my soul was stirred within me, and I couldn't stand it any longer. I knew it was my duty to do all I could to reach these poor fallen creatures and bring them to God, and thus check to some extent the devil's work; but it now seemed to me that some one ought to strike at the fountain-head, and break up those miserable dives. I went to ——, and he referred me to his agent, ——, and from him I went to a number of others. I was all stirred up, and I could not sleep nights. I would toss on my bed, listening to the hideous sounds from the streets below—cries, groans, mad laughter, and broken snatches of songs, with occasional cries of ' Murder!

murder !' At daylight I would start out again to see if something couldn't be done to stop up these heli-holes—the
cause of all the trouble. I received plenty of promises, and
that was the end of it ; until, finding I had worn out a pair of
shoes and received no help, I became hopeless of doing anything in that way, and went for them the best I could on
my own hook, trusting in God to strengthen me and give
me success: and he did, until I kept the police headquarters
so warm they hated to see me coming, and would say when
I came with a new case, 'There comes that McAuley again.
Who in the world has he got *now ?* '

"The policeman who was now stationed on that beat soon
began to let us know that his sympathy was with the rum-
sellers and dives. His name was Savage, and he was rightly
named ; for he was as great a savage as ever I saw. I had
thought nothing could be worse than Fitch had been, but
this brute was worse than all. When he couldn't think of
anything else to worry us, he would walk into the Mission-
room—in direct violation of his orders—while the meeting
was going on, and stamp over to where we had a little shelf
on which a Bible and a newspaper or two were usually found,
and stamping as hard as he could with his great heavy boots,
he would pick up a newspaper, throw it down again, and
stamp, stamp, stamp, all the way back to the door, and if I
would go for him, he would get out before I could get at
him. I was standing in the door one night, while he stood
outside with some of his friends, and finding he could not
get in to disturb us without passing me, he commenced
grinning to one of his pals. 'Ah, I'm not going to look
after his ould Mission,' said he, after throwing out a number
of other slurs.

"'Why, of course,' I answered good and loud, ' of course

you won't ; but if I'd sling you a *couple of dollars* occasion-
ally, as all these *miserable gin-mills do*, you'd watch for me,
wouldn't you ? '

" He grated his teeth savagely, and dropped his hand to his
club like a flash ; but I started towards him, and looking
him square in the eyes, said : ' If you *dare* to touch *me* with
that club, it'll be the last job of the kind you'll ever undertake ! You haven't got that *poor woman* to club to death
now ! '

" He started back astonished, and soon left me to myself.
My blood was up, for I had in my mind a case which I will
tell you about, to show what a brute he was and what kind
of encouragement the poor fallen ones sometimes receive to
help them to reform.

" One of those poor unfortunate girls, under the influence
of liquor, and not knowing what she was doing, wandered
out on the street and created some disturbance by singing.
Savage went for her, and began clubbing her with his heavy
night-club. It was not daybreak yet, and everything else
was so still, we could hear her screams, and distinctly count
the heavy blows of that terrible club—thug—thug—thug—
like pounding a great ox. I could not stay in bed, so, running to the window, I looked out to see if I could catch him
at it. There was a great pile of mortar opposite us, where
they were building the new houses, and just as I reached the
window he struck her and knocked her down into the mortar. She stretched up both hands at arms' length, begging
him not to kill her. He struck first one arm and then the
other with his club, and they dropped, as if broken by the
blows. He then beat her out of the mortar and across to
the curbstone on my side of the street ; when, as she made
one more effort to regain her feet, he knocked her down

with another blow, and she dropped on my cellar-door. I dashed up the window, and called to him, ' Hold on there! Why don't you take that woman in, if she's done wrong? What do want to kill her for, say ? '

" ' What's that your business ? ' he answered, as soon as he recovered from the surprise caused by hearing my voice.

" ' I'll show you in the morning,' I retorted. ' Now you take her to the station-house, or I'll make you pay dear for your brutality to a helpless woman.'

" He picked her up, and started around the corner with her, and I went back to bed. I learned afterwards that she became so weak, no doubt from the clubbing, that she couldn't walk ; so he called another policeman like himself, and when they found her unable to go without being carried, they fell to clubbing her again, first one striking her and then the other ; and those who heard it said her screams were ter-rific.

" A man was clubbed to death on the same beat about this time, under very suspicious circumstances. Part of Savage's beat was travelled during certain hours of the night by a Dutch policeman. The latter, on going over his beat one morning, found, he said, the body of a man who had un-doubtedly been clubbed to death and then thrown behind a box. Savage blamed it on the poor Dutchman, and of course it would not do for me to say the former did it, as I had no personal knowledge of the fact. I take no pleasure in referring to these painful memories, but in order to rightly understand our struggles at that time, you must know some-thing of the obstacles we had to contend with, many of which were actually brought in our way by the very ones the city was paying to protect us! During all this time the meet-ings were going on first rate."

But opposition was not confined to the minions of the law. Those who do not know the kind of stuff of which our hero was made may wonder that the work was not given up in despair. But besides having a fast faith in God, he was possessed of great personal courage, and opposition only served to keep his enthusiasm stirred up. At the same time, in speaking of those days of difficulty, Jerry invariably attributed his success to God. These are his words: " It was a tremendous struggle to carry on this work under such difficulties, and as I look back to those stormy times I see the mighty hand of God leading and supporting me through it all. If it had not been for his all-sustaining grace I should have quit and got out of that wicked locality as fast as my legs would carry me, but he sustained me so fully that I did not even think to myself of giving up the fight. There was a special policeman detailed to look after the Mission at night, but he soon proved as much an enemy as any, until I took his number and complained of him, and he was moved out of the ward.

" The meetings continued to do good during all this time. The Lord poured out his blessing, souls were saved, and the devil seemed to grow more mad every day. Seeing they could not get the best of us while we were looking at them, the rabble tried some new tactics, and would wait quietly until the meetings were started and going, when they would smash the windows. Some one would be praying or talking when crash would go a pane of glass. This continued until there was hardly a pane of glass left in the house. We wired them up then and left but one exposed; this being toward the back of the building, near where the organ stood, had thus far escaped the fate of the others.

" The meeting had commenced one afternoon when bang

came a brickbat through the window, close by the musician's head. 'Oh,' he exclaimed as the brick whizzed past him, 'what's that?' 'Oh, that's nothing,' I replied quickly; 'they send whole paving-stones sometimes; that is only a *piece* of brick!' 'Hallelujah!' cried out one of the audience; 'let them come! The Lord is our defence, so they can't harm us!'

"It was about this time that the houses opposite being finished, they were thrown open for tenants, and a man named Johnny Wagstaff—a wretched fellow—moved in. He came with two big car-loads of furniture, and strutting around made all the show he possibly could. As he was about to go into the house with the last lot of goods some old acquaintance standing outside spoke to him, and he turned laughingly and said, 'Oh, I thought I'd come down and keep *Brother* McAuley company.' We hated to have that rum-hole there, for we had prayed God that no such place should ever prosper there. We kept on praying, and Johnny found us a thorn in his flesh, for we cut off his customers and hindered his sales. He fought hard, and was determined to beat us anyway if possible. I shall never forget one Fourth-of-July night. They had made up their minds to fix me and the 'Ould Mission' that night anyway: so they procured an old barrel and placed it in the middle of the street; they then set a watch at the door, and as soon as any one rose to testify they lighted a *pack of fire-crackers* and dropped them into the empty barrel. Of course with the terrible racket they made a man couldn't hear his own voice. This seemed to promise to be a great success and break up the meeting entirely, and would have done so if a happy thought had not helped me out. After we had tried several times in vain to hear

each other, I said to the congregation, 'Now I want you
to watch me : I'll select a hymn ahead of the time, and the
moment I say " *Sing!*" just sing with *all your might*, and when
I say, " *Testify!*" be ready and spring right up.'   A convert
arose and opened his mouth, when bang! bang! bang!
went the fireworks in the barrel. 'Sing!' I shouted, and
they fairly roared ; my! what lungs they had, and you
couldn't hear those old fireworks at all!   Just as soon as
that pack was out I called ' Testify!' and a brother jumped
up, and before they could get the next pack ready and
rightly on fire he was through, and then we drowned the
racket again with a grand old hymn.   I knew they could
not keep this up forever on account of the expense, and
soon they quit it and began to fire their roman candles at
the back of the house ; but we kept right on, and we never
had a better meeting.   It was certainly a lively one all
through, and as one expressed it afterwards, ' We had a
red-hot time.'   Several were helped spiritually, and among
others one soul was *gloriously saved!*   Johnny grew poorer
and poorer, and after a while his trouble increased daily,
and at last his wife died and he gave up.

   " He came into the Mission, and I shook hands with him
and talked to him kindly, He soon moved out, and it
wasn't much trouble for him to move *now*, for instead of
his car-loads of furniture he had only an *old scuttle partly
full of coal!*   He died shortly afterwards, and the place was
again ' To let.'   We carried the matter to God, and prayed
him to break up whoever came in there to sell rum ; and
that prayer was heard, for fifteen or sixteen failed one
after the other and moved out—several having lost all their
money trying to do the devil's work in that place."

   Of another occasion Jerry speaks as follows :

" A friend whose gifts were given by the wholesale had charge of the meeting on the night in question, and stood with the open Bible in his hand reading.   I had not reached the chapel, but was on the stairs coming down.   Mr. A. had just finished a sentence, and was about to read further, when a fellow let out an unearthly yell—like an Indian— ' Silence,' he shouted ; and Mr. A., who had never heard such an awful sound in his life, jumped as if he had been shot, and nearly dropped the Bible from his hands.   I came in a second after, and couldn't think what was the matter. My wife kept nodding to me and pointing at the giant of a fellow who roared so.   I didn't know anything about it— though I could see something had happened ; but out of respect to the Book that Mr. A. was now reading again, I asked no questions.

"In a moment or two we were startled by another un- earthly yell, and I walked down to where this man sat. He was a perfect giant, with great, broad, massive shoulders, and his red shirt being open at the neck showed the heavy matted hair on his breast, making him look like a lion.   I spoke to him kindly, and told him he would have to be good or go out, and informed him that we always insisted on good order.   He pointed over his shoulder to his chum sitting behind him, as much as to say that it was he that created the disturbance ; but I paid no attention to his motions, and kept on talking to him.   I then went back to my seat, determined to keep an eye on him.

"Mr. A. went on with the reading and pretty soon I saw this bully drop his head, and in another minute he uttered that terrible yell for the third time.   I knew I was in for it now, for if I let this fellow get the best of us our last hope of ever going on with our meetings undisturbed

5

would be gone. I thought of this, and then I looked at him, and knew that a row with such a great brute of a fellow was no joke; but the work of the Lord was at stake, so I walked down to where he sat and told him firmly he must leave.

"'Ah, go on!' he growled. 'What's the matter wid you?'

"'Come,' I answered quietly, 'you must go out, or I'll put you out.'

"He looked at me a moment, but made no move to do as I told him. I then reached out and caught him by the collar, when he coolly threw his arms over the back of the seat, locking his hands together with a grip like a vise, and said, with a grin, 'Go ahead, old fellow.' I suppose he thought I could not lift him. I ran my hand down to get a good hold of his shirt-collar, and surging back, I brought him to his feet, bench and all. I dragged him out into the aisle, but he clung to the long bench till one end of it suddenly struck the ceiling and that broke his hold. I grabbed him by the throat now, as he struck at me square from the shoulder and tried to hit me between the eyes; but he soon found out that I had not forgotten all I knew of the 'manly art' when I stopped his blows cleverly, and in return gave him another shove nearer the door, tightening my grip on his throat all the time.

"He kept hitting at me like a madman, but failed every time to get a blow home on me, while in the mean time we were getting nearer and nearer the door. When not striking at me he would clutch at anything and everything —the benches, the heads of those near him, whatever he could get hold of—trying to stop his progress.

"I felt the God of battles was my helper, and I was bound

to win. It was like a battle between the kingdoms of good and evil. By the time we got to the door we were in such a fearful struggle that when we struck the doors—about two inches thick, and built of hard wood—we carried them clear off the hinges, and split one door all up. By this time he was black in the face from my grip on his throat, and he gasped, 'Let go! l-e-t, g-o! I'll be-have; l-e-t, g-o, J-e-r-J-e-r-r-y.'

"'Ah,' I said, as I gave him one more squeeze and a tighter one, and shoved him off. 'Ah! ah! you great old coward, you're *no man* after all!' He begged hard, and I let him go. When we got out on the sidewalk where I had dragged him, I found it had been a put-up job; for across the street stood a lot of his chums shouting, 'Give it to him, Jackson. Give ould Hallelujah Jerry fits;' but they did not try to help him. 'He won't give it to him, nor you either,' I replied.

"As soon as Jackson caught his breath he ran across the street where there was a new building, and he and some of the rest picked up bricks and prepared to brick-bat me. I didn't give them time, but walking coolly over to them I said, 'Ah, you cowards, drop those bricks—drop them!' and they did, and ran for their lives. I then saw two policemen standing looking on and laughing at them.

"I then returned to the Mission, and joined in singing 'Rock of Ages, cleft for me,' which they had been singing all through the row. Things went on about as usual after this, but the would-be disturbers were a little more careful for fear of meeting with a similar defeat, for this man Jackson was one of the worst men in that worst of streets.

"After a while, however, another disturber came in and thought he would try a new trick on me. He made some disturbance, but I saw he had been drinking, and said, 'Don't mind that poor fellow, friends; he has been taking a little too much gin.'

"'Not a drap of gin, Jerry,' he replied. 'Nothing but good ould bourbon whiskey.'

"I saw he had got to be bounced, so I started up a good hymn and went for him; when he saw me coming he laid right down on his back on the floor, thinking I couldn't get him out in that position. It may be he had heard how I put Jackson out, and took this way of getting the best of me.

"'All right, young man,' says I; 'if you prefer going out that way, I've no objections;' and taking him by the collar on the back of his neck I dragged him down the aisle and out he went."

CHAPTER VI.

MORE ABOUT WATER STREET.

"Put thou thy trust in God,
In duty's path go on,
Fix on His work thy steadfast eye,
So shall thy work be done."

Some idea of the neighborhood in which Jerry worked is necessary to a right understanding of the nature of the task upon his shoulders. We have quoted already some of his words in reference to his surroundings. Upon another occasion he thus describes them:

"But few can have any idea of the terrible dens with which this wicked locality was crowded. The basements were especially loathsome, several having particular names, such as 'The Well,' 'The Man-trap,' etc. They were merely holes in the ground under the houses, where the tide backed in twice a day at high-water. In each of these dark holes, without any window or outlet, with no sinks or anything in the form of an opening, for any purpose whatever, except the entrance from the street, from four to six girls or women and as many men used to live. From these death-holes the girls would come out and button-hole men as they passed by; sometimes they would snatch the hat from a sailor's head and dart back into their den. If he was wise he would keep right on and let his hat go, for if fool enough to go inside it would be the worse for him; he would most likely be thrown out after being beaten and

robbed, if not murdered, for sometimes men never came
out of those holes alive. The inmates of these filthy dens
died off rapidly, but their places were filled right away by
others.

"This terrible state of things weighed on my mind so that
I could not sleep at night, but tossed restlessly upon my
bed, and I felt that to clear my conscience I must do something to break up these fearful places. I found to my
astonishment that the owner of the property where these
places were kept was a very rich man living on Broadway,
and was considered a very nice, respectable gentleman. I
went to him with my burden, but he paid no more attention
to me than he would to the barking of a dog. I could not
for the life of me understand how this fine gentleman could
be so indifferent to things that seemed so terrible to me.
My astonishment was not so great when afterwards I found
out that each of these holes brought him in from $30 to
$40 per month!

"Seeing that it was no use to expect anything from this
man, I next applied to a well-known Society, and laid the
matter before the agent. The latter was very enthusiastic,
and told me with perfect assurance he would attend to it
right away, 'and he would soon have Water Street as quiet
as Fifth Avenue.' Encouraged by this I went home and
waited to see what they would do.

"I was becoming discouraged again when I didn't see
anything of the tremendous clearing out that had been
promised, until one day on looking out of the window, I
saw some policemen standing near the curbstone on the
opposite side, staring up at the Mission. My first thought
was that the Mission was on fire, so I walked over and inquired, 'What's the matter? Is it on fire?' 'No,' one of

them replied, ' we were sent down here to watch the Mission.'
I looked at them in astonishment; to *watch the Mission*,
while here in broad sight, and within a few feet of them,
these wicked wretches were robbing and plundering everybody they could get hold of.

"' Why,' I exclaimed, as soon as I could control myself,
' I didn't want any one to *watch the Mission*, but I want to
break up these dens around here ! ' ' Oh, we've got nothing
to do but to obey orders,' was the cool answer; 'and all
the orders we got was to come here and watch the Mission.'
I finally went to another temperance man, paid him some
money, but with no better results; but by this time I was
learning how to attend to the matter myself, so having
received some money from Mrs. Dr. Barnet and another
lady, and adding to it the little I had, I went to work.   I
selected some of the converts to get the proper evidence as
witnesses, and then would bring the parties into court, and
having good clear testimony to actual offences committed,
I secured convictions, and thus broke up these dens one
after another, until they became as scarce as they had once
been plentiful.

"But it was no easy matter, and I had to contend with a
bitter opposition, not only from the proprietors of the
places themselves, but from their friends among the lawyers
and others holding official positions ; judges, lawyers, and
some of the police authorities began to go for me, but
knowing I was in the right, I fought on.   A lawyer, whose
name has been before the public a good deal lately, kept
me on the witness-stand for two hours and a half at one
time, insulting and abusing me, in trying to clear a man
named Dugan whom I had arrested.   The facts of the
case were as follows :

"This fellow (Dugan) kept a dive, and I went in and demanded to see his license in order to secure evidence in this way that he was the proprietor. The bar-tender replied, 'The license is locked up in the safe, and can't be got till the man who has the key comes in.' I knew this was a trick, for the law demands that the license shall be hung up in a conspicuous place, where anybody can see it. I waited patiently, until one day, while standing at the door with the policeman who was to be stationed at the Mission, I saw Dugan enter his dive. I spoke to the policeman, and asked if he would go over with me. 'Certainly,' he replied, and over we started. We had almost reached the door when he suddenly stopped and refused to go any farther.

"'Why, what's the matter?' I asked.

"'Oh, I don't want to get into a muss, for Dugan is a friend of the inspector, and he'd go for me.'

"'Ah, you old coward!' I replied; and there I was, the laughing-stock of the whole crowd of ruffians and degraded women who were looking on. I was not defeated, however, in the attempt to arrest him, for shortly after this I had him taken up and brought before the judge, and that was the time when I received the rough handling from the lawyer.

"I not only had to put up with the abuse of the lawyers and others, but was bothered with repeated intentional delays. The case was called several different times, but each time there was some pretended reason for laying it over: twice or more they pretended that Dugan was too sick to put in an appearance, and thus the thing was kept up to worry my life out. My lawyer failed to do his duty, so in the end I lost the case.

"Shortly afterwards Dugan was really taken sick, and growing worse, it looked as if he was going to die. I knew how he hated me, but I also knew he was now sick and in trouble, so I went over and knocked at his door. ' May I come in?' I asked kindly ; ' I don't want to intrude on you, but would like to come in if you will let me.' He recognized my voice, but nevertheless he answered faintly, ' Yes, come in if you want to ! '

" I entered, and after talking with him and his wife a short time, I knelt in prayer. I prayed earnestly for them, and held them up in the arms of faith to a sin-pardoning Christ, who never turned one poor trembling soul away, and who loves even his enemies, and would do them good. They were both very much broken up, and wept freely, and I left.

" Encouraged by my first visit, I called again, and brought a beautiful, sweet bouquet of flowers. Again I called, and this time managed to secure a few peaches, they being very scarce at that season of the year, and brought them to him. He seemed to appreciate my kindness, and was more broken up than ever. We talked over matters, and, referring to his business· of his own accord, he said he was very sorry he ever engaged in the rum traffic at all: knew it was wrong, but once in he could not get out without losing everything he had, and this he had not the moral courage to do while in health and strength. He lingered a short time, and died from exhaustion."

In all the history of our brother's work it is most inspiring to see that the more and the fiercer the opposition, the more did God honor his labors. So he speaks as follows of one of these seasons of bitterest opposition on the part of the enemies aroused :

" Meanwhile the work of soul-saving went on with wonderful success, and God's presence was manifested more and more. There would be as many as twenty-five or thirty forward for prayers at one time, while the aisle would be crowded with those unable to get seats. Still the meetings increased in interest and attendance until, there being no room inside, the people gathered around the door on the street. We could not find standing-room for more than half of those who wanted to get in.

"The revival took effect for a while among the captains of the Baltimore freight-boat line, and became of considerable interest. One captain by the name of B—— was converted, as were also all of his crew excepting the cook.

"One night his engineer, having heard from others, came to see for himself what was going on. The captain was there that night seeking help, and before the meeting closed the engineer became deeply convicted and knelt to ask God to forgive his sins. While we were all on our knees some one whispered to me that Captain B. and his engineer did not speak to each other. 'Is that so?' I answered, and getting off my knees I went to where he was and whispered :

"'Captain, you must be an *awful* hypocrite?'

"'Why? How so?' he replied in astonishment.

"'Because you claim to be seeking the Lord, and yet you won't speak to so-and-so over there, and are holding hatred in your heart. *Shame on you !*'

" He dropped his head, and leaving him I went softly over to the engineer and whispered the same words to him. It was but a moment when they both sprang to their feet at once, as if moved by the same impulse, and meeting, fairly hugged each other, and wept, and then knelt down together and cried to God for forgiveness. They prayed earnestly for mercy, and the captain was the first to receive the answer. He clapped his hands, and the joy was beaming in his face. But he had hardly time to straighten up fully when the engineer also caught the joyful sound of forgiveness and was on his feet in an instant ; and then they began shaking hands and hugging each other again.

"The Spirit of the Lord had touched them, and all their enmity and hatred had vanished like the dew before the rising sun. Others soon caught the spirit, and gathered around them, shaking hands and rejoicing, shouting and weeping with them, until some of the outsiders ran across the street, thinking the old Mission was tumbling down.

" I asked one of the boatmen who was saved at that time, when he was testifying, ' How do you know you were converted?'

" ' Well, I'll tell you,' he replied; ' I went from here to my boat, and locking the door, just made up my mind never to open it until converted. *And I kept my word!* '

" ' How could you tell when it was done ?'

" ' Well, I'll have to explain that in my own way,' he answered, ' but it seems to me the Lord just took, as it were, something like a barnacle-scraper [a keen, sharp-edged, three-cornered piece of steel, fastened to a long handle and used to scrape off the little shellfish and other deposits that gather on the bottom of vessels] and *scraped my heart all out clean*, and I haven't felt anything wrong there since ! '

" Another came forward, and I asked him to pray for himself.

" ' I can't. I don't know how,' he replied mournfully.

" ' Oh yes, you can—just say the Lord's Prayer.'

" ' I don't know it.'

"' Did you never hear it?'

"' No; I've heard about it, but I never heard *it*.'

"' Well, just pray in your own way. Ask the Lord for what you want in your own words.' He bowed his head, and in a moment broke out, 'O Lord! O Lord! scratch my sins out, and then *keep them scratched out!*' and the Lord answered that simple but honest prayer."

These stories of redeeming grace might be multiplied a hundredfold had full records been kept, but Jerry appears to have had little care for making up grand totals. When souls were saved he gave God the glory, and was encouraged to go forward in efforts to win others, leaving the record to be made up in heaven. The few cases that follow in these pages are illustrative of many more.

"One night," he says, "we had a wonderful meeting; a Catholic girl was earnestly seeking salvation. She had pleaded and prayed for forgiveness for a long time without experiencing any change, while the Spirit of God seemed to hover over that congregation and every other prayer was stilled in awe, as all present listened breathlessly to the simple but deep and fervent petition of that poor girl. She actually seemed to talk to God face to face, with a holy reverence that subdued every listener and hushed every doubting thought. All at once she ceased praying aloud, and bowed her head in silence upon the seat, while a peculiar hush rested on every heart, as if expecting a quick answer. After a moment's silence she slowly raised her face toward heaven, and, with hands outstretched, whispered distinctly, 'He is *coming!* HE IS COMING!' bringing her hands together in triumph as she uttered the last word. Her prayer was answered, her faith accepted. She made no farther demonstration for a moment, and nothing could be heard but her deep breathing and the subdued sobs of some others kneeling near her, while they actually trembled so that the rattle of the bench at which they knelt could be distinctly heard, in spite of their efforts to hold it still. This girl became a remarkably earnest and devout worker. It was really wonderful to witness her faith and her success in reaching others, especially women, and bringing them to Christ. She remained faithful, and removed to the far West afterwards, where she continued an efficient and highly esteemed Christian worker.

"It was about this time that an Irishman who had worked for McCreery & Co. of Broadway came to us. He was a remarkably handsome man, and came of a wealthy family of consequence in Ireland. He was dissipated and almost a wreck, when a trip to this country was proposed, to remove him beyond the influence of his old associates, and thus reform him. But change of place is not a change of heart, as was soon shown in his case, and new comrades of similar habits are not hard to find in America, when a person has a little money to share with them in debauchery.

"He grew worse until his father refused to send him any more money to squander, and in this condition some one brought him to the Mission. He was led to seek the Lord, and was soundly converted. He kept up a correspondence with his father, who soon discovered by the general tone of his letters that there was some remarkable change in his boy for the better, and after a further trial he received him to his affections again, and sent him money with which to return home in joy and restored confidence. He came and bade us a tender good-by, and said he expected to have one of his father's houses opened and run as a Mission similar to the Water Street Mission, as soon as circumstances would permit."

CHAPTER VII.

TROPHIES OF GRACE.

"Welcome, welcome! sinner here!
  Hang not back through shame or fear;
  Doubt not, nor distrust the call;
  Mercy is proclaimed to all.

"Welcome, weeping penitent;
  Grace has made thy heart relent.
  Welcome, long estranged child;
  God in Christ is reconciled."

" Another remarkable incident occurred about this time. A gentleman from the West, afterwards the editor of the *I—— Record*, came to New York on some mining business. Being a drinking man, he drank to excess, spent his money, neglected his business, and at last he became so reduced he could not raise the price of a drink, or even a meal to keep body and soul together. Famished with hunger, he wandered down to the Battery, where he saw a crowd around a street-preacher. Anything was better than to be alone, with the craving of the rum appetite, the gnawing desires for food, and the lashings of his conscience, as he thought of the cheerful home and loving, trustful wife who was expecting his return, while he was wandering here a penniless, deserted drunkard. He went toward the gathering and took his seat on one of the benches. He listened a while, but felt no interest. Finally it seemed he could do without food no longer, and turning to a dirty tramp who sat on the bench beside him, he asked, 'Say, where can a fellow get something to eat? I'm dead broke, and have had no food for several days.' The tramp turned toward him and said, 'Why, don't you know! Why, go up to Jerry's, of course! it's a big lay-out about ten o'clock Sunday morning. All the *bums* here take it in, I tell yer! Yer get a *good* bowl of soup and a chunk o' bread; and say,' he continued, as he smacked his lips in anticipation, 'the soup's got meat in it *too !* ' He had no choice now, so getting the directions from his new acquaintance, he came to the Mission. I saw him as soon as he entered, and picked him out as a peculiar case. He carried a cane, not worth pawning, and though he bore every mark of dissipation, a judge of human nature could see in a moment that he had seen better days. I walked up to him and received him cordially, treating him as a visitor; shook hands, spoke pleasantly, etc., as if I didn't know he was dead broke, and in want. He looked at me and said, 'Say, I'm hungry; won't you give me something to eat?'

"I took him up to the corner of the table, gave him a knife and fork—the rest had to go for it with their fingers—and in half a minute the bowl was empty, and bread, meat, and all were devoured. I filled it the second time carelessly, pretending not to notice his hunger.

"After he had eaten sufficiently, I talked with him about his soul. I was deeply in earnest, and he felt it, and finally broke down, wept, and prayed. He then told me his story, 'Oh,' said he, in tears, 'I'm a man that has a happy home, and a loving wife with a dear little child. I have not written home, and they have no idea where I am. I came on here to see about some mining stock, but I fell into bad company and took to drinking, and all my money is gone, and I dare not write home now.' He did not get clearly saved, though he made some effort in that direction. He left off drinking, and telegraphing home, his wife sent him $100 to return to Michigan with. I bade him good-by, and shook hands with him as he left to take the train ; but alas for him! he concluded to take one drink, thinking it no harm if used in moderation ; and the first, as usual, demanded a second, and he remained in the city, and his waiting wife and child were disappointed in their expectation of father's return. He became beastly drunk, and after a short spree found himself penniless and friendless again. In despair he went and enlisted in the navy, thinking in this way to bury himself from the eyes and search of all his friends, and at the same time be placed where he could not get hold of the cause of all his trouble—the cursed rum. His wife waited patiently for him ; but failing to see or hear anything of him, she could stand the suspense no longer, and came to New York to look for him.

" She searched in every direction, but failed to find him ; and then, remembering that his address had been 316 Water Street, she almost gave up all hope, for on inquiring. she heard that Water Street was the lowest, most wicked street in the whole city. Almost broken-hearted, she came down to the Mission, and supposing from what she had heard that it was a bad house, she trembled to come in and make any inquiries. She decided, after waiting as long as she dared, to take a look in at the windows anyway, and shading her eyes with her hands, she peered in through the glass, and was struck to see right before her eyes two mottoes, ' Have Faith in God,' and ' Stand up for Jesus,' on the wall. 'Surely,' she thought, 'this *can't* be a bad house; and she finally mustered up courage enough to come inside, and not seeing her husband, to inquire of the janitor. ' Does Mr. M—— live here.'

" ' No ma'am,' replied the person questioned ; ' he did stop here, but has gone home to his family out West.'

" ' When did he go ? ' she asked fearfully; the man answered, and she knew from the date mentioned that he would have reached home weeks before she left there if nothing had happened, and with a stifled moan she sank faint-like on a seat.

" The truth now burst upon her mind that he was again on one of those fearful sprees. No one could tell her where—in the city, or in some railroad town along the route from here to her home ; no one could tell her, whether in prison or out, whether dead or alive ; who could know? She thought of this, and then of her deserted home and little one so many miles away ; and heart-broken, hopeless, and worn out, she burst into tears. As soon as she could control herself sufficiently she told him who she was, and then we came in and did what we could to comfort her.

" She began a diligent search for her poor drink-enslaved husband, but for a long time it was all in vain. She employed the best detectives she could get. In the mean time she knelt, burdened and sin-sick, at the feet of Christ, and was gloriously saved. ' Just think of it, coming 1500 miles to get converted ! ' she exclaimed. Surely God moves in a mysterious way. She continued the search without getting any track of her husband, until, becoming completely discouraged in all human efforts, she took it all to God in prayer and left it with him.

" She was about to start for home, when Mr. M—— was discovered in the Navy Yard. Steps were immediately taken

6

to get his release, and they were surprised to find so little opposition from those who knew him there; but we soon learned that it was because his melancholy and despondent state of mind unfitted him entirely for any service; and not only affected him, but his comrades also, to such a degree, they too were made homesick. He became a nuisance, and they were actually glad to get rid of him with his blues.

" The devoted wife went after her repentant husband, and as soon as they could get to the city they came direct to the Mission, and bowed together before God. Such a sight was scarcely ever seen on earth; and as the poor fellow, amid the sobs and prayers of his wife and the rest of us, gave his heart to Christ, we felt assured there was joy in the presence of the angels of God.

" He returned home with his now happy companion, and we soon heard that his business had proved a success, and was bringing him in a great deal of money; his prosperity proved too much for him, however, and he fell from his Christian profession. He remained in a backslidden condition but a short time, and returned to the Lord again, was fully recovered, and remained so to the hour of his death, when he passed over in the full triumphs of faith.

" His happy death was an evidence of God's wonderful power to rescue the poor drunkard from the grip of sin, and clean him up for heaven."

Among the many marked and memorable trophies of grace was a man formerly known as " Rowdy" Brown, the name perhaps sufficiently indicating the character of the individual. But so far from marvelling that such a man should be saved, we remember that grace saves the lost. Our divine Redeemer only vindicates his name as such, and illustrates the nature of his mission on earth, when he saves those lowest sunken in the degradation of sin. "Rowdy" Brown's story is thus told by Jerry:

"About this time there occurred one of the most remarkable events of our history. There was a certain man called 'Rowdy' Brown, a great, powerfully-built, courageous fellow, who was a terror to the Fourth Ward. He had been a mate on the Liverpool packets, and was a savage brute. He hated religion and everything belonging to it. Once he happened to see a man sitting on the forecastle reading his Bible, and without a word or sign of provocation, Brown drew back his heavy boot and kicked the poor fellow square in the mouth, knocking his teeth out, and disfiguring him cruelly. He went to California once, and while there, it was reported, killed several men. We always receive such rumors carefully, knowing how things grow and are exaggerated by travelling from one to another; but there was probably some truth in the stories, for when questioned by me he did not deny them, and in fact acknowledged that there was something in it by explaining to me how some of the cases occurred.

" He seemed utterly fearless of consequences to himself, as he proved by standing one day cursing a man to his face who stood with a revolver in each of his hands, and fired both their contents into his body. That's the kind of man Rowdy Brown was.

"He was stopping at Mr. Rhody's new Sailors' Home, when he was told that one of his sailor chums was converted at the Mission. He was mad when he heard of it, and swore a big oath, adding, 'I will take a bottle of whiskey down there, and when that feller gets up to talk, I'll take him by the upper jaw in one hand and the lower jaw in the other, tear his mouth open, and pour the whiskey down him or break his back in the attempt.' And *he meant it*, and was capable of doing it.

"I did not know of his threat or of his coming, or I should have been on the watch for him. He came armed with the black bottle, and waited for his old companion to testify, in order to carry out his plan. While waiting he listened, and listening, became interested, until all of a sudden he felt a strange feeling coming over him, and he began to tremble. He fought it off with all his natural obstinacy, but it was no use: it continued to grow stronger, and when his friend arose to testify, this human lion was as tame as a lamb. When the testimonies were ended, and sinners were invited to come forward, Brown stood up and called out 'Oh, pray for me!'

"Everything was in a state of quiet but intense excitement in a moment, for many present knew his desperate character. We gathered around him, and how he cried for mercy! It was awful to hear that man groan and beg! His strong body was racked with the anguish of his soul. He continued seeking in this manner until the meeting closed, but apparently with but little encouragement. On the second night, after getting into his bed, he was praying earnestly, when suddenly the light broke into his heart, and he knew the work was done. He jumped out of bed, and soon aroused his mate who slept with him, with his shouts of praise to God for his pardoning mercy. He became a diligent worker, and sometimes in his earnestness would go out on the street, pick up a poor sailor, and almost haul him into the Mission. When the invitation was given to those anxious to be saved to rise for prayers, he would put his arm under theirs and fairly hoist them up. Melted by the burning, loving prayers, many a man would weep and yield himself to be saved.

"Brown was liberal with his means, and often on his return from a voyage he would give us fifteen or twenty dollars at a time to help on the work.

"How he lived his religion aboard ship and among his associates can be best told by relating the following incidents: He shipped on one occasion, after his conversion, aboard the West India brig *Nellie;* the captain was ashore one day while at Matanzas, and met an old acquaintance, a captain also, whom Brown had formerly known and in fact had beaten unmercifully a few years before. After a few minutes' conversation the captain of the *Nellie* remarked, 'Captain, do you know who is converted?'

"'No, I don't.'

"'"Rowdy" Brown.'

"'What!' exclaimed the other, looking at his friend as if he thought him crazy, '*Rowdy Brown!*' then adding slowly, after a moment's silence, 'I don't believe it.'

"'Well, he is, all the same, and is aboard my brig *now!*'

"'I *can't* believe it,' continued the doubter. 'Do you know he gave me a most unmerciful thrashing once, besides cutting away my brig another time? He was a *devil;* he *can't* be converted.'

"'Yes, sir, he is,' insisted the first, 'and he is going to have a prayer-meeting on board to-night. Come and attend it, won't you?'

"The other made no reply, but seemed completely bewildered by the astonishing news he had just heard, and they parted.

"'Rowdy' Brown had fixed up the deck of the *Nellie,* and had a great canvas stretched for an awning, with a sign paint-

ed, bearing in large letters, 'JERRY McAULEY'S PRAYER-
MEETING HERE THIS AFTERNOON AT THREE O'CLOCK.'
He would run the boats backward and forward, and bring
off loads of sailors to the meeting.   A revival broke out, and
spread among the crews of the different vessels. Gentlemen
and ladies also from the shore, who were from the United
States but were living there, came aboard and became
deeply interested in the meetings.

"One day 'Rowdy' Brown went ashore, and, meeting a
sailor he knew slightly, asked him to come to the meeting.
The man showed a bitter, hateful spirit, and replied, with a
sneer, 'No, I *won't!*'   '*Do* come, oh do!' said Brown
earnestly; and yielding to a sudden impulse, before the
man could reply he fell on his knees, and with eyes filled
with tears, begged him to come to Christ.   The man looked
at him for a minute, but hardening his heart against those
strange pleadings, growled, ' No, I won't go: I've been to
McAuley's in New York, and he couldn't convert me, and
you can't neither.'

" Brown declared, on meeting some of his Christian helpers
directly afterwards, that as soon as that man said those words
all interest for him left, and he had a strange feeling as if cold
water had struck him, and arose from his knees, wondering
what it meant.   The next day the man who so bitterly refused the offers of mercy was working on a scaffold over
the side of his vessel, when suddenly he was missed by
some one who wanted him.   The *scaffold was empty;* and
though the vessel was searched, he could not be found.
Shortly afterwards his body was discovered through the
clear water, lying face downward with his mouth in the sand
at the bottom.   He was fished up, and a black bottle,
partly filled with liquor, was found in his pocket.   He

probably became drunk, and fell off the scaffold into the water. It was a strange affair, and so affected his shipmates, who seemed to think it was the voice of God in a fearful providence, that they became serious, and the captain of the vessel, with his entire crew, were brought to the Saviour.

" From the last account we received from Brown he was doing well, had secured some property in Canada, and was living a consistent Christian life. Later on we heard of his death, and had every reason to believe he died in the faith."

CHAPTER VIII.

A MISTAKE AND WHAT CAME OF IT.

> " Sow in the morn thy seed,
>   At eve hold not thine hand ;
> To doubt and fear give thou no heed,
>   Broadcast it o'er the land.

> " Thou canst not toil in vain ;
>   Cold, heat, and moist and dry,
> Shall foster and mature the grain
>   For garners in the sky."

Before us lies a copy of the " Report of the Helping Hand for Men, 316 Water Street, for the years ending October 1873 and 1874," from which brief extracts have already been made. It is of itself an interesting document, and bears upon its cover the words of the Lord Jesus, " According to your faith be it unto you." Interest is added to the pamphlet by reason of Jerry's trial of faith in connection with its publication. We will let him tell the story in his own words.

" About this time (October, 1874) something happened that proved how God will take even our ignorance and blunders and make them to glorify him, if we are only honest in trying to serve him. It was thought best to get out a report of the Mission in order to let people know what we were doing. We could not afford to get out an annual

report, and so we had to make one for every two years answer. This was rather new business to me, and consider-
ing it a big undertaking, I thought it ought to be done on
a large scale. So I ordered *ten thousand copies printed !*
When I spoke of it to the others interested they were taken
all aback, and were almost indignant. '*Ten thousand copies !*
Why, Jerry, *what* are you thinking about ? Where is the
money to come from to pay for such an amount of printing?' Of course I felt bad, and I told them it was new
business to me, and I had done the best I could. They
acted as though they felt that my being sorry would not
pay the bills, and were only half satisfied.

"In my trouble I remembered Him who had never failed
me when I trusted Him. So I said, 'Well, never mind : I
have faith the Lord will send some one to pay it.' I
was determined now to make the best of it, and that as
long as we had them on our hands to pay for they should
not be idle ; so after considerable thought I struck a novel
plan to use them. I persuaded Brother Charles Anderson
to help me, and we went up-town on a pilgrimage to get
them among the churches. We started out, each with a
great pack of reports on his back, to fulfil our mission
We failed to lighten our burdens at the sanctuaries, with,
I believe, but three exceptions—Dr. John Hall's, Dr. William Taylor's, and Dr. Booth's churches, where they let us
leave some. I approached the sexton of Dr. Hall's and
told him what I wanted, and begged him to assist me. 'I
want you to assist me,' I said ; 'you know we are poor and
trying to do good, yet hardly able to live along ; by just giving your consent to let me lay these in the pews before the
people come you may do a great deal of good.' He made
no objections after a little, and going in I distributed them

in the different pews, and took my departure, leaving results with the Lord. The next day a carriage drove up to the Mission door and two ladies stepped out. I had been praying for help, for I thought I had done some terrible thing and was awfully burdened over getting the little Mission in debt. As I saw them entering my heart jumped up into my throat. Faith said, 'There's an answer to your prayer.' No, thought I, that can't be, for they have not had time to read the reports yet, unless they did so while the doctor was preaching or as soon as they reached home, which did not seem likely.

"They came in and began to talk with me, and I saw from their words that they had seen the inside of the pamphlet. They handed me fifty dollars each and departed, refusing to give any names. I was happy—'What a miracle! *One hundred dollars!* Whew! Three cheers!' said I, hardly able to hold myself in; 'we're safe now. Here's the money. Hurrah!!!' I needn't add that my wife and I had a little praise-meeting all by ourselves right away.

"A young lady named Miss S——, a member of Dr. John Hall's church, also found the report in her pew, and turning over the leaves carelessly saw something that attracted her attention, and, as she told us afterwards, she soon became so interested she didn't get a word of the doctor's big sermon, and before the meeting closed she made up her mind to come down and see for herself. She got an escort, and came to the old tumble-down Mission. After attending a number of the meetings she became very deeply interested about her own soul's salvation. One Sunday night she was there, and we had a wonderful meeting: the Lord bared his arm there that night in power; everybody felt it, and there were many tears and sobs as God touched heart after heart in that room. While the meeting was in progress, Miss S—— slipped a beautiful cluster diamond-ring from her finger, and at the close of the service she passed it quietly into my wife's hands, and whispered earnestly, 'Here, Mrs. McAuley, take this and sell it for the good of the Mission. Do pray for *me*, won't you? I'm an awful wicked sinner!' We were surprised; such a beautiful, well-dressed young lady '*an awful sinner!*' and coming to be saved! Why, that was worth more than all the diamond-rings in the world! We talked with her the best we could, and she said as she left us that she would call the next evening about tea-time.

"She came as she promised, and after some talk about spiritual things she knelt down alongside the old sofa and we prayed for her, and before she arose she gave her heart to Christ. All she could say was, ' I'm *very* unworthy, but if the Lord can condescend to take me, I will take him as my Saviour.'

"She arose from her knees simply trusting in the Lord. The hour for meeting had now arrived, and as we started to go down-stairs to the chapel she said, 'You *must not* ask me to speak in the public congregation; if you should, it seems to me I should faint.' 'All right,' I answered, 'if you faint, I'll have some one ready to pick you up.'

"We went into the chapel and I opened the meeting. I had scarcely had time to sit down, when we were all amazed to see Miss S—— jump to her feet, and with glowing words testify to Christ's power to save. The Lord blessed her in the act, and blessed her testimony to the good of others. She has continued faithful, and has acted in an efficient manner as a volunteer missionary wherever she has resided since. The ring, we were afterwards told, cost her three hundred dollars, but the Lord gave her the signet-ring of adoption, worth a thousand times more than all the diamonds in New York.

" About this time in our history a professional gambler named William Fitzmorris, supposed to be the inventor of the envelope game, came to the Mission. He had been keeping a gambling house up-town, but according to his statement, had to come down so heavy to keep on the right side of the police, that his business would not stand the strain. So he moved into a new place in a basement, and stationed three men at different points as lookouts, to keep the police from coming on him unawares—finding it cheaper to keep three men under salary than to pay the blackmail he had been paying before.

" A certain notorious policy-dealer offered him three dollars a day to write policy-slips. How wonderfully God works, and how little we know what is to come of our plans! Fitzmorris accepted the job, and came down to see about it. Standing on the corner he saw our lamp, and asked somebody, ' What's that ? ' ' Why, that's Jerry McAuley's. You ought to take it in ; it's as good as a theatre.' He came in to see the fun, but became interested, and the testimonies melted him all up and he came forward, knelt down, and was saved. He gave some fearful descriptions of his terrible business, and the scenes he had witnessed while engaged in it. He told how men of families would come in and stake little by little their earnings until every cent was gone ; then, fascinated by the game, they would strip off their clothing piece by piece until they could go no farther ; of the young girls sent by mothers to buy policy-slips for them,—sent into these hell-holes, amid the cursing and obscenity of the loungers there, by their own mothers,—until step by step they began to be crazed over the game and would buy for themselves. From an ex periment it grew to be a habit, from a habit it became a passion, and in the end they would sell themselves to get money to gamble with.

"His revelations were published in the daily papers, and his old associates became so enraged that they threatened to kill him.

"We kept him with us, however, and thus protected him from their fury. His health continued to fail, and we expected soon to have the sad task of laying him in the grave; but his friends came and took charge of him, and by his consent removed him to their home. He got no better, and it was plain to all that his end was near. He did not fear death, but continued strong in his faith, and clear in the assurance of his acceptance with God through Jesus Christ. Finally, when almost gone, he made a request to be carried to the dear old Mission, where he had found peace to his poor soul, that he might there testify to the precious love of Christ once more. Finding his heart was set on it, his friends consented, and he was brought in a carriage to the Mission, and there, held up on his feet by a man on each side of him, he gave his dying testimony.

"It was a wonderful time! It seemed as if we stood on the steps of Heaven, and you couldn't hear a breath. He stood and, with feeble voice and shining face, every word of convincing power, gave his last testimony : 'I know I am *dying ;* I *know it*, and because I know it I came here to give my dying testimony, to speak once more in this hallowed spot ere my tongue is silent forever.' You never can put on paper the tones of his voice or the effect of that wonderful scene. No one who was there will ever forget it."

Tidings of the old Water Street work have gone out into all the earth, and fruits of grace gathered within its walls are to be found in all quarters of the globe. The audiences from night to night had always more or less of a transient nature, and while often persons living close by despised the place, men and women from afar found in it a beacon-light, directing them into the haven of eternal blessedness. Still at times gems for the Saviour's crown were gathered at its doors. Some of the neighbors were converted, as the following story will show. Jerry in his record says:

"The converts were not from among our neighbors, but were mostly visitors, wanderers, sailors, etc. One or two neighbors from across the street finally ventured to drop in. One case is well worth repeating. One night a beautiful little child about five years old came to the door. She was a lovely little thing, with bright blue eyes and long golden curls—a perfect little picture, notwithstanding the poor care she had received.

"She turned to the man at the door, and asked, 'Say, Mister, won't you please let me in? I'll be good if you will.' 'Oh no,' he said, looking down at the little waif; 'you couldn't behave.' 'Yes I will; I'll be awful good, 'cos I want to hear the singing.' He yielded to her entreaties, and she went in, and folding her little hands on her lap sat as quiet as a mouse until meeting closed.

"The next evening she came again, leading by the hand another little girl, younger than herself, but looking very much like her. She again asked permission to go in, and having referred to her good behavior the previous night, it was granted. They walked deliberately up to the very front seat, and lifting her little sister well up on the bench, Mollie sat down beside her, and closely watched everything that was said or done. They behaved beautifully, and at the close of the meeting my wife kissed them both, and then gave them a chunk of cake each, and they ran out happy enough. This happened several nights, and they always got their kiss and cake.

"One night during the meeting the mother of the little girls came to the door drunk, and asked if the children were there. The man replied he thought they were, when she said, 'I'll be thankful to ye, Mister, if ye'll go in and kick them two children out.' 'We don't do things that way here,' said the man; when she called 'Mollie, Mollie Rollins, come out here!'

"Poor little Mollie turned pale and trembled, and looked at me with such a frightened look, like a scared bird. The mother screamed out her name again, and added, 'I'll give it to *you*, going in there with those black Protestants, you little wretch;' and as poor Mollie came out, dragging her little sister after her, the drunken mother caught her by the beautiful curly hair, and flung her clear off the ground. 'I'll kill you if you go in there again,' she screamed. 'Do they give you any beer in there, say?' The poor little thing looked up, though the tears were in her eyes, and said: 'O mamma, ain't you awful! they don't drink any beer in there, and they don't get drunk neither!' The next night, just as service commenced, in walked Mollie and Jennie again. 'Ain't you afraid your mother will kill you?' we asked. 'Oh no,' she answered quickly, as she turned her blue eyes up to my face; 'I ain't afraid. I like the *singing*.' Everybody around the Mission loved those darlings, and was pleased to have them there. We missed them for two or three evenings, and afterwards learned the father had returned from a sea-voyage. The husband and wife both went on a terrible spree with the money he brought, until finally he brutally turned the mother and little ones out of the house into the cold October night-air.

"That night, about eleven o'clock, Mrs. McAuley heard her name called. She listened a moment, and recognized Mollie's voice calling from the street, 'Mrs. McAuley, O Mrs. McAuley, come down. I want to tell you something.' After a minute the little voice rang out again: 'Mrs. McAuley, O Mrs. McAuley.' On going down, my wife learned that the father had put them out, and they had been on the roof. As the wind blew cold, the little one said to her mother, 'Mamma, I know a place where the wind won't blow, and where we won't be afraid.' 'Where's that?' asked her mother. 'Over in the Mission,' said the child. My wife came upstairs, saying to me, 'Mrs. Rollins is there with her children. I have let them in; I believe it may be the salvation of that woman's soul.' We took them up-stairs, where we had the only accommodation the old Mission-house afforded. It was a rickety affair, but was the best we could do. There was a straw tick there, and a few old quilts, and as they turned in Mollie looks up to her mother and says, 'Thank God, mother, we have a *good* bed *to-night*.'

"In the morning we gave them their breakfast the same as we had ourselves, and sat with them at table. We never mentioned anything to the mother about her conduct, but treated them kindly, and after breakfast they left. This was the first step towards reaching that poor woman, and it turned out that the little acts of kindness were not lost.

"The man having spent his money, went off to sea again, but left the family his advance-money, and this was the mother's opportunity for another big spree, and she made the most of it. She spread it everywhere, and soon the money was gone. But rum must be had, and one thing after another went to the pawn-shop, till there was nothing left that would bring a penny. The poor children were dirty and unwashed, and their hair was all matted and tangled, and they looked fearful. They came in one day, their lips blue with the cold. My wife warmed them and then washed them, combed out their hair, and curled it beautifully over their foreheads. She then begged two little dresses from a friend who had some small girls; the dresses were somewhat worn, but were neat and clean, and the dear little things were happy as larks. When they went over where their mother was drinking, she hardly recognized them. 'Oh,' said she, 'what happened you? Who did that?' The rum-seller's wife remarked, 'Why, I'd never known them!' 'Nor I,' said the mother; 'I hardly knew them myself; well, you look good, anyhow.' This was the second blow on that hard heart.

"Shortly after this, the long spree began to tell on Mrs. Rollins, and she was taken sick, and after suffering awhile, she sent Mollie over after my wife. This being the first move towards us she had ever made, we hailed it with joy. My wife went as requested, accompanied by a friend, and oh, what a miserable sight met their eyes! The room robbed of everything movable but the remains of a bed, fragments of broken dishes scattered all around the dirty floor, the room cheerless, fireless, comfortless. The dishes that were not broken were dirty and piled every way, while the stench of the neglected room was fearful. They found her stretched with the horrors (delirium tremens) and without saying much to her, straightened up the room, made a fire after getting some coal, and then the friend went home and brought over a big pitcher of good strong hot tea, and told her to drink it, which she did in a hurry. This helped her somewhat, and they talked to her about her condition, and pointed her to the Lamb of God for help, and prayed with her.

"These acts of kindness were the hardest blow of all to her prejudices, and she broke down and said, 'If ever I get well of this spell I'm going to come over, Mrs. McAuley, and see you at the Mission.'

"She got well, and one night she came into the Mission during the meeting. We were singing the 'Stone rolled away,' when she screamed right out, and starting from her seat, ran through the kitchen, thinking to get out that way. My wife followed quickly and caught her, and then kneeling down beside her, prayed earnestly with the poor sobbing creature. She found the Lord's help, and He so sweetly saved her, that it was apparent to all.

"At first she used to put an old shawl around her head and draw it well over her face, and then go around the block before entering the Mission, to keep the neighbors from recognizing her; but afterwards she would walk straight across the street to and from her home, singing the 'Stone rolled away.'

"She was bitterly persecuted, because she was a turncoat as they termed it. Her door was broken in, slops were thrown over her, and they even caught the poor little children and beat them, hoping to enrage her, and thus make her return to drink again.

"The errors of her past life began to tell on her, and she became very ill with consumption. The people she had spent all her money with would not do anything for her, and we took her to Dr. Cullis' Home for Consumptives in Boston. We went with her, and left her in the good doctor's care. She grew gradually worse, until almost at death's door. She had a dream or vision one day, in which she thought every one had forsaken her: even we had ceased to love her, and God had forgotten her, but suddenly she heard a voice, 'I won't leave you. I'll be with you all the time.' And she was encouraged. She also thought that Mrs. McAuley stood by her bedside, and she felt relieved. Dr. C. wrote us to come on if we wanted to see her alive, and we went immediately to Boston.

" My wife walked in and stood by the bed, and when the poor invalid opened her eyes she smiled faintly, and said, 'That is just where I saw you stand,' and she reached up and clasped her poor bony arms around my wife's neck, and oh! such a scene I never witnessed before. I could not stand it, and went out of the room and let them sob away ; but I heard her murmur, 'Oh how I love you both! I love you better than my own children.' This more than paid us for all our efforts. The next day she passed over in the triumphs of faith and redeeming love. Before she died she expressed a desire to visit that place in Water Street where God spoke peace to her soul, and added, "Dead or alive, I want to be under that blessed roof once more." In accordance with this wish, her body was brought on to the Mission for burial.

" There was a very large turnout to the funeral services, and a stranger gathering never was seen. There were present many ladies and gentlemen from the first circles of society, and there were several of Mrs. Rollins' old comrades, some of them dragging their children with them to get a last look at the face of their late acquaintance. Many of those parents were confirmed drunkards of the lowest type, and had entered this Mission for the first time in their lives ; yet all this seemed forgotten in the presence of the dead."

CHAPTER IX.

EVIL SCHEMES FRUSTRATED.

" Their hearts shall not be moved
    Who in the Lord confide ;
 But firm as Zion's hill,
    They ever shall abide ;
 As mountains shield Jerusalem,
 The Lord shall be a shield to them."

While possessed of a native shrewdness which, sanctified as it was, helped him much in his work, Jerry did not forget to seek for wisdom from on high. But for this he would no doubt have been deceived to his cost again and again. As it was, the Lord cared for his servant, and the well-planned devices of the enemy were constantly frustrated. One or two cases Jerry thought worthy of record, and they are appended.

"We have met a great many frauds while engaged in this work, but the greatest of all—the very Queen of frauds—appeared in our history one time, and I have no doubt if the Lord himself had not overthrown her designs a terrible reproach would have been put upon both my wife and me, and we might have been entirely ruined and our work broken up.

"We were down at Asbury Park for a few days' rest when this creature came upon the stage of action. Brother and Sister S. had been to their regular services at the John Street Church, and were on their way home to Williamsburg, when they thought they would stop into the Mission for a few minutes, inquire after our health, and get a drink of ice-water or lemonade. They had talked awhile with the janitor, and were just going away, it being after ten o'clock, when there was a sudden rap at the outside door. When the janitor opened it he found a fine-looking young woman standing there. He let her in, and then the visitors listened to her story.

"The girl stated that she was homeless and friendless, and being at a loss where to go had stepped up to a policeman, a few moments before knocking at our door, and inquired of him where she could find a respectable night's lodging. He did not treat her properly, she said, and turning from him she raised her eyes and saw the Mission. She knew she would be safe with Christian people, and so without hesitation knocked at the door.

"Her previous history was a sad one, and our friends listened to it with the deepest interest and sympathy. Her father, she said, had been wealthy up to a short time before his death, and when he died he left her $3700 in care of her brother, who was older than she was. The brother became intimate with the son of a rich gentleman where he boarded, who was a fast young man and soon led him into dissipation. His constitution, not strong at best, gave way under his excesses, and he went into hasty consumption, and soon died. Just before his death he gave his sister's money to this young associate to turn over to her. The man promised faithfully to carry out the dying request of his late comrade, but as soon as the latter was laid in his grave he went on a long spree, and kept it up until the money was all gone, his own health broken, and he also brought to death's door.

"When he died all hope of ever getting her money van-

ished, as the father refused to be held for the debt. **In this**
condition she wandered around until she knocked at the
Mission door for protection.   Mr. and Mrs. S. were greatly
interested in her story, and when she concluded they proceeded to find a place where she could stay until morning,
as it would not do, on account of the speech of the people,
to leave her there alone with the janitor for the remainder
of the night.

" After a great deal of trouble they found accommodations
for her and went home.   She paid her own bills, and afterwards got a boarding-place in Monroe Street, and came to
the meetings every night.

" We came home about this time, and supposing, as a matter of course, they had investigated the matter, we took her
into our confidence and did all we could for her.

" My wife felt a little uneasy sometimes about Jessie, as
she called herself, and then blaming herself for her sus-
piciousness, treated her more kindly than before.

" My eyes began to be opened after a while by some of her
actions when off her guard.   Once when my wife and I
were talking about coming to Thirty-second Street to open
the Cremorne Mission, the girl overheard us, and exclaimed,
without thinking, ' Oh, good ! I'm glad of it ; I'm *well acquainted* up there around the Cremorne Gar——' She
caught herself suddenly, but her prudence came too late.
I was looking her square in the eyes, and saw her confusion
like a flash.   I said nothing, however, until she left the
room, when I turned to my wife and remarked, ' She is
from that neighborhood after all.'   This put us on our
guard, but we feared to do her injustice or hurt her feelings
by showing any suspicions until we were certain that she
was playing a game.

"She came running in one day shortly after, and appeared in great glee as she exclaimed, 'Oh, good news! good news! I've got word from that father, and he is going to pay me back, with interest, the full amount his son squandered for me! I'll tell you what I'll do,' she continued excitedly, 'I'll give it *all* to you to start that mission up in Thirty-second Street. Won't that be grand?' I heard her words, saw her earnest and apparently honest manner, and she seemed so enthusiastic and generous, I began to believe in her again, and to scold myself for my suspicions. Of course I was glad to hear her offer of the money, for I was then very much exercised about how I was to get the means to open the expected mission up-town. I intended to put a mortgage on a little property I owned, and put in all my own available cash, with what I could raise in other ways; but all this would be far too little for even a fair start. Here, thought I, is the whole thing all worked out for us! I now proposed to myself to accept her offer, and secure her by the proposed lien on my property until the first anniversary, when it would be an easy matter to return her the money again with interest. The skies looked all bright again for my proposed Thirty-second Street Mission.

"'When will you go,' I asked her after a while, 'to receive the money?'

"'Oh,' she replied, 'in about three weeks from to-day I will take you and Mrs. McAuley with me, and we will go over and get it, bring it to Mr. H——, and take a receipt for it. We can then draw it as we want to.' After the three weeks had gone by, and she made no move to go after it, I asked the reason, and she answered, 'Oh, I've concluded to get it expressed to my boarding house, and then take it to the banker's.' I thought it strange that she would have so large an amount sent to a boarding-house, but held my tongue, determined to hide my sus-picions until the proper time. Shortly afterwards came the closing of the plot.

"She came in one evening, and told us the money had been sent over as proposed, and was now at the house in Monroe Street, all done up in envelopes. 'All right,' I answered; 'as soon as meeting is over we will go down and get it.'

"The meeting went on as usual, and after it was over we started out with her to bring home the *three or four thou-sand dollars!*

" We went together to the house, and leaving us standing on the sidewalk she went into the house to get the money. I felt a misgiving that she would not come out again, or that we were in some way having a job put up on us, and turning to my wife, as the front door closed upon our guide, I said, 'There she goes, and we will see her no more.' 'Yes, we will see her again,' was the positive reply; and sure enough, in a little while out came the lady with the packages of envelopes!

"'Have you got it?' I asked, when she reached the pave-ment.

"'Yes; it's here all right,' she replied. 'Here it is,' (handing a package to my wife). 'It's all done up correct, and in good shape.'

"'All right,' I answered, pushing the package back into her hands. 'You keep it, and walk ahead with Mrs. McAuley, and I'll follow close behind and protect you if needed.' The fact that she wanted one of us to carry the valuable package struck me as rather strange, and I was determined to be on the look-out for any plot that might have been cooked up to get us into trouble or entrap us, and then say we had appropriated the money. So, satisfying myself that my revolver was all right, in good condition, and handy if needed, I followed them slowly, watching carefully every dark alley and doorway, and every sharp corner, thinking that at any minute some fellow might spring suddenly upon us as we passed through that dangerous locality. The whole thing seemed so odd, that I felt pretty sure there was to be some strange ending to it all, for the idea had grown upon me that there was some deep-laid plot against us to injure our work, and I was determined not to be caught napping. Whether she was afraid to give the signal, seeing we were so fully on our guard, or not, I can't say, but anyway there was no attempt at harming us, and we reached the Mission in safety. Calling in one other as a witness, I turned to the girl and said:

" ' Now, Jessie, I want you to stand where you are and open those packages, and show us the money before this witness.'

" ' Oh, it's *all here!* ' she replied; and then fumbling over the envelopes as if examining their contents, she continued: 'Yes, it's all right—in checks—and you take it just as it is. We won't count it now, it is so late and we're all so tired. We can all come together the first thing in the morning, and count it out all right.'

" ' *Pull them out*, and count them now, before we go to bed,' I exclaimed, as I saw like a flash of lightning through the whole dodge. 'You can't leave that package in our care and then ruin us by swearing in the morning that we stole the money out during the night. Open them! quick!'

"She trembled like a leaf, and the packages on being opened were found to *have nothing in them!*

" 'Who put you up to that infernal trick?' I said to her sternly as I fixed my eyes upon her face. 'Come, out with it; whose plan is it? Everything else having failed, this was the last hope, was it?'

"She refused to answer, however; nor could we ever learn positively who was at the bottom of it. I shall always believe, however, that it was a put-up job. Thus did the dear Lord interfere again to save us from the plots of our unprincipled enemies, as He had done before and has so many times since.

"The girl, seeing she was caught beyond escape, got awfully scared at the prospect of arrest and imprisonment, and broke down, sobbing and crying like a child. She made some acknowledgments, but refused to give any names. She wept bitterly; and what do you suppose we did then? *Knelt right down there and prayed for her*, with our own hearts all melted up with gratitude to God for the wonderful deliverance He had just wrought out for us, and cared for her until she could get ready to leave."

Those who knew Jerry best will recognize him readily in the following incident, given in his words:

"A fellow came in one day shaking all over as if he had the palsy. He trembled like a leaf from head to foot.

" 'What's the matter?' said I.

" 'Oh, the *Lord* sent me here?'

" 'I don't know whether He did or not,' I returned; for he looked like a dead beat; 'did no one else send you?'

" 'Yes,' he answered slowly, pulling a dirty crumpled paper from his pocket, which he had probably carried about six months. I looked at him sharply, when he exclaimed,

'Oh, help me—I've got the horrors—I'm almost dead—*do* help me!'

"I pitied the poor fellow, so I took him in without further questioning, led him up-stairs and put him to bed, called a doctor, and did all I could for him. I could not do much with him spiritually, for he claimed to be a Christian and 'all right.' 'It is true,' he said, 'I drink a little, but they all do that where I came from.' He was taken worse one day and was so cramped that he was sure that he was going to die right off. 'Oh, oh,' he screamed, 'I'm going to die!' I knew he wasn't in a very bad way, so concluded to improve my opportunity.

"'Oh, you're all right, you know; you'll only go to heaven any way!'

"'Oh, but I can't die *so.*'

"'Oh, yes,' I continued, 'you can; it isn't hard for a Christian to die, you know!'

"'Oh, oh! help me! I'm dying!'

"'Why, you ought to be happy; why don't you sing?'

"'Oh! oh!'

"'It's glorious, *ain't it*, to be a Christian?'

"'Oh! oh!'

"'Why, my friend, you ain't scared, are you?' And so I talked with him in this way until he became ashamed, and then I said to him soberly, 'Now, my friend, you ought to get right with God. Just see how frightened you were when the first pain touched you. Oh, why don't you get saved?' I failed to get him out clear, though he claimed to be grateful, and made great promises of help to the Mission when he got well. One day he left, and we supposed he had gone for good, when a few days afterwards in he walked with a bundle of dirty clothes under his arm.   When I approached him he said:

"'Jerry, the Lord sent me to you to have these clothes washed!'

"'Did he?' said I.   'Well, the Lord sent me to fire you out;' and out he went like a rocket—dirty clothes and all."

CHAPTER X.

THE CREMORNE MISSION.

" E'er since, by faith, I saw the stream
  Thy bleeding wounds supply,
  Redeeming love has been my theme,
  And shall be till I die."

THUS far we have spoken only of Jerry's labors in the
Water Street Mission. For over two years previous to
his death he carried on a similar work in the Cremorne
Mission at 104 West Thirty-second Street. Of the origin
of that work he once said to a reporter :

" Dr. Talmage was the first one that started me to thinking about it. That was over two years ago. Dr. Talmage
had been around the dives and seen what was going on and
preached about it, you know. I had been around New
York some, and I thought I knew the worst places in it ; but
I was mistaken, for I'd never seen anything so bad as this
neighborhood. The first time I found out what it was
really like happened this way: There was a fellow they
called Happy Joe came up one night and got a little full,
and began to sing a hymn he'd heard down at our Water
Street place ; and at last he said, ' Let's have a Jerry
McAuley prayer-meeting, right here ! ' Well, the girls
jumped at the idea, and he took me off, and made fun of
the whole thing. Well, sir, that blaspheming rascal was
the cause of my coming here ! Those girls were so inter-

ested from his description that two of them came down to
Water Street in a carriage to our meetings, and then often
came.   One of them came to me afterwards and wanted
me to help find her sister, who had got into some bad place
up-town, she was afraid.   Mrs. McAuley and I got interested, and we came up to look for the girl's sister.   We
started in at Bleecker Street, took in 'The' Allen's, Harry
Hill's, 'Wes' Allen's, and all the rest there, and came up
and went to nearly all the Sixth Avenue dives.   Before we
got through I made up my mind that this was a worse
place than Water Street, and resolved, if the Lord would
help me, to start a Mission up here.   I finally fixed on this
place, because it was about the worst I could find."

Mrs. McAuley says : " We felt that our work in Water
Street was done, and the time had come when we ought to
make a change.   After this visit it seemed to us that the
cry went up to heaven for a mission here, that some of the
hundreds of young men and women frequenting these dens
and dives might be saved.   We went home and prayed God
if he wanted us up here to open the way ; and if he didn't
want us here to put up a barrier so high we couldn't climb over
it.   After many prayers and tears and with much fear and
trembling, we found a place.   Then we asked God if he
wished us to come, to send the means that day.   The answer
came, and soon we had $9000.   Then a number of Christian
gentlemen were invited to become trustees, and the place
was fitted up and the work commenced."

In June, 1883, Jerry felt led to commence the publication
of a journal which he named *Jerry McAuley's Newspaper*,
and which continues to be issued every month.   It contains
in its columns accounts of the Cremorne and other Mission
meetings in New York, with the testimonies of converts,

CREMORNE McAULEY MISSION,

104 West 32d Street, near Sixth Avenue, New York.

just as they are uttered in the meetings. From among these we have culled a handful of Jerry's own testimonies. It is to be regretted that more of them have not been recorded. Those of them in print we give without comment.

MISTAKEN PROPHETS.

I never undertook anything, but the prophets said, " Jerry, you've made a mistake." When I started the Water Street Mission, none of these wise fellows would come near me for a while. One man said : " Well, if it's a success, I'll give you $25." " Yes," I thought ; " *if;*" and *if* they were all like you it *could not be* a success." When I came up-town they said again, " Now Jerry has made the mistake of his life." Even some of the trustees objected, and said, " Water Street Mission will go down if Jerry leaves,"—as if Jerry McAuley was anything, or that God couldn't do without me. Not so. This Mission would just run on the same if I should die to-morrow morning. Why if any of you has the money I'll go and start a Mission right away at a place over here called " Hell's Kitchen," and another somewhere else, and they would all be full, and God would save souls. Now you want to tell the story just as it is—if God has taken you out of a dirty hole, say so.

COMMENCING THE WATER-STREET WORK.

When I first went into a meeting it was during the John Allen excitement. They asked whoever wanted prayers to stand up. " Well," thinks I, " them fellows can't hurt me praying for me;" so I stood up, and here I am to-day. I didn't go off to Harlem then, or some other place where no one knew me, to start a Mission and work for God, but I went right to work where I was well known.   I went to a certain minister, and he said:

"Why, you are wild, Jerry, to try and start a Mission down *there*.   Why, they'll kill you the first thing, and fire you and the old benches out doors together."

"Well," I replied, "let them! I've taken and given a good many hard knocks for the devil, and I think I can stand and take a few for the dear Lord Jesus; so I shall start right there where I am most needed, and where no one else wants to go."

"Well, go on then, if you must, and here is five dollars for you anyway, and God bless you."

And we went to work.   I got five or six of us up in one corner of that old house, and we roared away on "Rock of Ages," and "There is a fountain filled with blood;" that's all we knew.   We didn't know high metre from low metre, but we went at it with all our might, for we meant it.   No one came in for quite a while, when finally I discovered the reason: the old man I had at the door wouldn't *let any one in*.   He had the door locked, and kept them all out.   He wasn't going to let any of those bad characters in to disturb our meeting—not he.   We had some strange work, but see the results.   The Water Street Mission is alive to-day, with a number of branches in this country and in England.   The Cremorne Mission stands to-day as a branch of the old Water Street, and there are several branches from this one already.

CONFESSING FOR CHRIST'S SAKE.

There are a great many here to-night whom the Lord has made happy.   Many more have happy homes who at one

time had no home at all. We owe a great debt of gratitude. Just see what comforts I am surrounded with! See
my happy, comfortable home, see all the dear kind friends
I have now; yet this was not always so. I once lived a
crooked life, I am ashamed to say so, but for Jesus' sake I
confess it. It serves to keep me humble to refer to what I
was. It keeps pride down and crucifies the flesh. If we
humble ourselves the Lord says He will lift us up; but if
we exalt ourselves He will cast us down. If we lift ourselves up we will soon fall. Now, let each of you be
prompt to testify for God to the things you know of his
dealings with your souls.

THE STORY TO TELL.

Did you ever read in the Bible about that fellow in the
tombs? He tore all his clothes off and broke his chains, and
nobody could help him. But Jesus came along and saved
him, and put a new suit of clothes on him, shoes and all—
no second-handed things; but what did the fellow do?
Why, I expect he straightened up his coat collar and put
on a white choker and said, "Well, I guess, Lord, I'll go
along with you and have a good easy time, and folks will
think I'm respectable!" But Jesus said to him, "Go back
among the people that *knew* what a miserable old tramp you
were, and tell them what wonderful things God has done for
you." And I can imagine I see him go back and get up on
an old barrel, and tell the people what a miserable wretch
he was until Christ found him.

POWER OF TESTIMONY.

Some folks get wonderful pretty and precise, and afraid
to tell what God has done for them; and some poor listen-

ing soul, hearing these nice kid-gloved sinners talk, says to himself as he starts to go out, "They are a lot of pretty cranks, with their soft talk," when just then some honest soul will get up and say, "I was a hard case;" then the poor fellow going out stops and listens to catch every word; and as the man goes on to tell his story, the other sits down interested, gets all broken up, as he thinks, "That's just where I am to-night;" and soon the tears begin to run down his cheeks, and the next thing he is forward for prayers, then takes his place in the congregation to tell the old, old story, so new to him. Love testimony? [he continued.] I guess I do. That man there [pointing to Orville Gardner] came to prison where I was under sentence of fifteen years, and told how God saved him. I knew what he was before, and I got all broken up, and went back to my cell, got on my knees, and Christ saved me. Always give your testimony just as it is.

NO HALF-HEARTED RELIGION.

God has saved me. I was almost a tramp; but see the difference to-night. He has taken the appetite for that frightful rum away. I remember living in a basement over in Brooklyn without even a chair or a bed in it; in fact, we didn't have anything: yet He has taken us up, washed us, and made us clean in His own blood. A half-hearted religion won't do for me. I want something more solid, and this religion of Jesus Christ saves and keeps me.

A TEST THAT TOLD.

When I was in the old way, I remember one night stealing $100 worth of sugar from a schooner. After my conversion, one evening I was in Dover Street Mission, when who should come in but the captain of the schooner. He saw me, and asked those around "what they were doing with Jerry McAuley there?" They told him Jerry was converted, when he said, "he would rather believe the Devil was converted than McAuley."

They called me down to him, and the captain said, "Do you know me?" I said, "I think I've seen you somewhere." The captain replied, "I think you have. Do you remember the sugar you beat me out of?" "I really don't know," I said: "I've beat so many." He told me the circumstances; and then I said, "Well, I've been converted, and to prove it to you I will give you the $100." But he said he had beaten the owners and I had beaten him, and so we would call it square. I tell you, my friends, it pays to serve the Lord. I hope some poor soul may to-night conclude to be honest with himself and with God. Come on the Lord's side to-night.

FORGIVEN MOST, PRAISE MOST.

Those of us whom God has taken out of the dirty hole ought to be always telling of his goodness. It hurts me when God's people act as if they were ashamed to speak for him. I am no hair-splitter, and what God says to me I believe because he says it. You heard about the fellow who was describing a little fly to another friend, and he talked about the various parts of the fly, and so on, and wondered how they could have been produced, and "look," says he, "at this tiny foot. How could it ever have been made?" "Oh don't bother me," said the other. "God said, Let there be flies, and there was flies, and I know there is plenty of them, and that is enough for me." Some people are hair-splitters. "If I get religion, how will so and so come out?" Well, let God take care of that, and do you do your duty. He saved me several years ago, and he has kept me by simply trusting in him.

———

SLACK KIND OF CHRISTIANS.

I was thinking of what that lady who is seated over there said, when testifying to-night, about moderate-drinking and prohibition. It is a terrible thing to profess to be a Christian and still drink rum. Why don't all the preachers preach radical temperance? Shall I tell you? Because some of them dabble in the accursed stuff themselves! They sip it, and a few of them defend its use as a beverage (?), and call me a "lunkhead" and an "ignoramus" and "a poor, uneducated fanatic." Well, I'm willing to be called a fanatic in this matter, and I don't deny I am " uneducated " and an "ignoramus." I never pretended to be anything else; but this I know—*souls do get saved here*, and poor drunkards give up their drink and become happy, sober men, husbands, and fathers. Moody says, "God don't choose men according to their abilities, but chooses the man or woman next to Him; that is, the one who lives nearest to Him." Some folks don't know what it is to live near the Lord. They have no moral backbone, no strength of character, nothing in them for good or evil, and never will have. You ask them why they don't come to meeting, and they'll say, " Oh, it's too crowded up there at McAuley's," or " It's too hot up there at the Mission." I'd say to them, " I'm thinking you'll get a hotter place if you don't stir yourselves—a place you won't get out of easy, either." Here are ungodly men and women sweltering away every night, and these dainty professors think it's too hot. I wonder if the dear Jesus ever complained of it being too hot to help souls? These are the kind that won't take a stand for temperance or anything else. I don't see how you can put wine on your tables, or drink it yourselves, right in the presence of your children. May God help you to-night to see these things as they are! How would you like to give me a bottle of wine and see me rolling in the gutter, cursing and blaspheming the name of God instead of praying? Yet you are doing it to others who might be as useful. Young converts start well: God saves them from drink, and their homes brighten up; they get good employment, and begin to move in society. Again, they see your so-called moderation, and then say, " He is a good Christian man, and it can't be so wrong after all to use it in *moderation ;*" and he tastes, drinks, falls, and dies! Who's to blame? I know of an old woman down-town who no doubt commenced as a "moderate drinker," but when I saw her she was such a helpless sot that she soon after died through rum.

THE GREAT CHANGE.

I am glad the Lord has permitted me to live and to meet the friends of other years here to-day. I met Mr. H—— coming out of the bank once with $150,000 in his hand ; as he came out he took my arm, and I told him I'd have cut his head off once for half that amount. And I would; but see the change *now.* Here I am, with as good a suit of clothes on as he has! He carries a good watch, and, see there [pulling out his timepiece], so do I! I once couldn't sport a wooden watch. I speak this way, just to show what the gospel can do for a man if he will only be honest, and let God have his way. Why, I used to sleep on the dock, with a stringpiece for my *pillow !*

HE WAS CALLED A TURNCOAT.

The testimonies of this evening, [he said, huskily] will tell in eternity. I am sick to-night, and ought to be up-stairs, but I desire to see souls saved. I was taken sick first in Water Street, and grew worse while on my knees with the poor sinners crying for mercy, but would not stop until I got through. Then I crawled up-stairs on my hands and knees. That was my first attack of pneumonia. When I'm to die, and it may not be long, I want to die on my knees, praying for lost souls. I don't care how you bury me—any old box will do. I don't want any money spent on flowers for me. There are small fortunes spent on flowers at some funerals, and I think it would be better to give it to the poor. I would rather some poor soul that I was the means of leading to the Lord would put one little rose on my grave than have the wealth of a millionaire.*

My testimony to-night is, the Lord picked me up when I was a dirty tramp, without a friend or cent in the world. The Roman Catholic folks, who heard of my conversion, called me a "turncoat;" but I had no coat to turn—nothing but an old red shirt—when I came to Jesus.

HIS METHODS NOT APPRECIATED.

When I was first converted, I used to get up at every chance I got and tell the people I had been an old drunkard, and one of the trustees of the church didn't like it; and one said he wished I would not tell the people what I was.

---

* In view of Jerry's wish, here recorded, the incident mentioned at the close of Chapter XII. is peculiarly interesting.

We did not know how to put on airs, but went right in for solid work. We would go into the congregation, and talk to the people, and lead them to the altar.

One night my wife got a young lady to come, and we knelt down beside her to help her to the Lord; several of the pillars were sitting quietly on the platform doing nothing, and one of them, a "big gun," said sneeringly, "Jerry and his wife will talk that girl to death." Wife heard it and arose and took her seat, but I didn't hear a word; and 'twas well I didn't: just as wife got up, the Lord wonderfully saved that girl. Oh, how happy she was! It was a good thing we did run the risk of talking her to death, for she died shortly afterward, and went over in the triumphs of faith, and is now "safe in the arms of Jesus."

TAKING UP THE CROSS.

I hope all the converts will feel the responsibility that rests on them to-night. If you feel it's too heavy a cross for you to bear, you ought to ask God to take it away. I used to think it was a terrible thing to talk in meeting and tell what God had done for my soul. At first when I used to get up there would come a great lump in my throat that nearly choked me, but I would jump up and hang on to the seat, and say "I love Jesus," and flop down as if I was shot. I always felt better for it. Let every one improve the time to-night.

CHAPTER XI.

ANOTHER CHAPTER OF TESTIMONIES.

"Saved by grace, oh, blessed tidings,
    Wonderful His love to show,
Jesus died to bring salvation
    To the perishing below.
        Saved by grace, through Jesus' blood
        Made an heir and child of God !"

NOTHING TO BOAST OF.

WE, the converts especially, are responsible for this meeting. It depends on us whether it proves a success or · failure. If we keep still, nothing can be done ; but if we do our duty promptly and keep in the Spirit—speaking and singing as God wants us to—this meeting will be a success. Most certainly is this true of those of us whom God has taken out of the lowest depths. Some seem to think if a man gets up and tells how low he was, "a poor forsaken drunkard," "a miserable thief," etc., that he is boasting of his shame. I tell it here often, and yet it hurts me every time ; hurts me right here [he continued, pointing to his heart], and I can't get rid of it ; it may be pride, but whatever you may call it, it's there ! For Jesus' sake and for his glory I'll endure the shame, and tell plainly what he has done for my soul.

Now I want you all to testify and tell what God has done for you, and be as short as you can. You have, probably, all heard about the three men with the pot of stir-about, haven't you? Three hungry men had a pot of stir-about set before them, but had only one spoon, and the stir-about being too hot to use their hands, one was to use the spoon and then pass it to the second, and so on. Now what would you think if one fellow took the spoon and kept it all the time and let the others starve? Well, pass around the spoon. The meeting is open now for testimony. Don't you see it?

THE PRODIGAL SON.

I read that scripture about the Prodigal Son a long time ago, and I thought I was like one of those characters, and I thought the other didn't have much religion either! Why, he got mad when the poor wanderer came home, and then went off growling and grumbling. He was one of those nice, goodish boys who brag about always staying at home and taking care of everything—very nice, precise folks—kid-glove sinners; but they are usually like this fellow—not half as good as they think themselves to be: for here is your never-did-wrong chap growling and getting mad at his poor old father, and it don't say the Prodigal ever did *that!* What did he growl about? Why, because the father loved his own child, and was glad to see him coming home after staying away so long—was glad to see him even though he was in rags, barefooted, and heart-sick! There are some of those steady brothers around yet. Well, I praise the dear Lord I am his child to-night.

NOT ALL FROTH.

I am saved from being a drunkard of the worst kind. I was a gambler and led a crooked life for years. I was brought back to Christ in what was called the "John Allen excitement." It may have been *an excitement*, but it was not all *froth* after all, for I was saved there, and I know of others in Water Street who were saved, and lived saved afterwards. I love God to-night, and I love precious souls. I saw a poor man here to-day with the shakes, fighting against rum, and I pitied the poor fellow with all my heart. I know if he holds on to God in prayer he will come out all right. I've seen it done often before this. Now let any one testify to what they know to be true in this Christian life.

NO REPROACHES FOR SINNERS.

Jesus saw Zaccheus up in the tree and he knew him, knew all about him; but I notice he didn't call him an extortionist, or a robber, or any hard name, but merely said, "Come down, Zaccheus; I'm going to take *dinner* at your house to-day!" Didn't accuse him of anything. He never does. Never calls those who come to him hard names! . He never called one of those poor unfortunate women a "Magdalene" once—*not once in his whole history.* No, sir! The bigger the sinner the more tender Jesus was. He never was harsh, only with one class of people—those hypocritical Pharisees; those dead church-members who professed religion, but hated Christ, and were only hypocrites. He went for them; and so he ought, and so do I go for them, and I intend to keep it hot for them. I praise Jesus for the wonderful change he has made in my life in the last few years. It would make a wonderful picture to paint me as I was when I first came to God, and as I am here to-night. He cleansed me inside and out.

TWO YEARS OF PRAYER.

A friend who came to the Mission a skeptic, but was at length converted, had given his testimony, when Mr. McAuley rose and said :

"That testimony did my heart good, not simply because the speaker referred to me or my prayers, for I don't know as they had anything to do with his conversion. It might have been in answer to the prayers of some of the godly men and women who come here, or it may have been my wife's prayers. I cannot tell. We did pray for him, it is true ; and to be honest with you, I got discouraged over him. I thought him one of the hardest cases that ever came into those doors. Think of it, two years praying steadily for one man before he yielded !

"I can say to-night I am saved by the tender mercy of God. I owe all I have to-day to Him—home, friends, and everything. I love the Lord to-night for all he has done for me. The meeting is now open ; let the time be improved."

ABOUT CONFESSING.

"I don't see," said he, "how any one can get over, under, or around that verse about confessing. Some people say ' It isn't our style to stand up and speak ; we don't do that sort of thing in our church.' But there stands the Word of God ; and I tell you the testimony of Orville Gardner in State's Prison was the means of bringing me to Christ. I had heard preaching there for seven or eight years without its having any effect upon me at all, because I had no confidence in the minister. We must be honest with God. My prayer to Him is that He will keep me honest. It's not the way I talk before you, but the way I live, that must tell."

FELL DOWN, BUT DID NOT STAY DOWN.

In the early part of my experience I stumbled a great
deal, but God saw I was honest, and he helped me over
the rough places. I will have to acknowledge, for I hate
hypocrisy and I can't help hating it, and won't be a hypocrite myself, that I became discouraged once or twice in the
beginning, and let go of God and went back into sin. Yes,
I went back to the *rum and all,* but I didn't stay there.
I came back to the Lord again, and He forgave me; and,
seeing I was determined to be honest and true, he blessed
me again, and has kept me ever since. The trouble with
some men is they have no backbone, and if everything don't
go to suit them, they let go, fall, and stay there. If a man
knocked one of you down would you stay there and let him
kick the life out of you? No! Of course you wouldn't—
you'd get up and try and save yourself, wouldn't you?
Well, that's the way to do with Satan: if he gets you down
by some foul blow, don't you lie there and let him kick you
to death, but jump up and strike out for yourself!

NOT IMAGINATION.

We used to have our trials too. The devil would torment
us, and men and women too, would revile us and call us
"turncoats," etc. One fellow said to me, "O Jerry, you
only imagine yourself into it; the whole affair is just the
work of your imagination."

"Well," I replied, GOOD for *imagination !*"

"Well, that's all it is!"

" All right," I said, "I used to be just like you are *now,*
wretched, ragged, friendless, homeless and unhappy; now
see me, I am contented; have a good conscience and every-

thing I need. Say! why don't you imagine yourself into it then too? It's so e-a-s-y, and it's certainly *better*. Just imagine it, why don't you?" No, my friends, it is not all imagination, but you can all prove it for yourselves if you will, to-night.

NO ONE TOO BAD.

The Lord is good to me; if I had my just deserts I would not be here. I tell you, I believe that if ever God left anybody outside the gate it would be me. Since I found mercy I know that none can be too bad for the Son of God to lift up, and cleanse, and save. Did you ever know Jesus to speak a harsh word to a sinner? The worse the sinner, the kinder the Lord Jesus was.

THE SOUL BENEATH.

I suppose I was the first one to open a place for tramps, and we would have as many as fifty or sixty at once to provide lodgings for; they would be stretched out on the benches and then on the floors, until there was not room to put your foot down without stepping on them. They were a terribly degraded set—hungry, ragged, and alive with vermin; but we looked beyond all that, and saw only souls for whom Christ died and whom he desired to save, and every now and then God found a real jewel among them.

When I first started out I had a pretty hard time, and I expected I would. Some people seem to think the Lord is going to send a convoy of angels and float them off to heaven as soon as they are converted; but that's a mistake. It wouldn't be good for us if it was so, for we'd never grow in grace one particle.

SIGHTS NEAR THE SEA-SHORE.

I'm saved to-night from everything that's wicked and bad. I was down to the sea-shore to-day to attend a Sunday-school gathering. On our way home the train stopped at a station, and a crowd rushed in until every inch of room was taken up, and *such* a crowd! Men and women, old and young, and the fumes of their breath were sickening —regular bucket-shop rum. Just think of it; men and women too, with flushed faces, reeling brains, and with their breath so offensive with poison that it would knock a decent man down! They had not been crowded in but a few moments before the atmosphere of the car was unfit for a hog to breathe. Yet these were men and women made in God's own image! I am glad I am saved from being a drunkard and a public nuisance. God will save every one, if we will only get honest, and come to him for help on our knees.

Let all do their duty to-night, and remember the one-minute rule. Some one said a few nights ago, in speaking of this one-minute rule, that there was "no liberty here." Such fellows want to get up and take up the whole time themselves, spinning it off by the yard, and then they'll go off and say, "Oh, we had *such liberty* down at McAuley's." Yes, but they had it all to themselves: no one else had a bit! Now, let all speak short and to the point.

GETTING RID OF "THE BLUES."

The meeting is open for testimony. We will never see *this* night again. May the Lord help us to testify for him, for we may never have another opportunity! Some come here night after night and always keep still, never speak at all. I often think if God's cause here depended on you, it would be a poor affair. Some folks come here with the blues, they say, and can't talk. Why don't you get rid of them before you come here, or else get up and confess, and get blessed? I often come when I feel like lying down in the aisle, I feel so bad ; but I see the need of putting forth an effort to rescue poor perishing souls, and so I ask God to help me, and do the best I can. Don't you know the Lord takes a worm sometimes to thrash a mountain ? I am saved to-night from everything wicked and bad. I was once without a friend, without a home, without God, and without a hope for either world ; now I have all of these, and have had for fourteen years. Some good people think that God can't save a blackguard ; but if you will come here often, you will be wonderfully disappointed when you see some that God saves here ! I was once one of the dirtiest, drunken, fighting old tramps you ever saw. God converted me in an instant ; I never swore an oath since that day, nor knocked a man down—that is, in anger ; I used to have to carry them out on my shoulder down in Water Street Mission ; but what I claim is that God takes the ugly fight all out of a man when he converts him— don't make him a coward, but takes away all desire to harm any one else. God always makes a way of escape for us. I have had men draw back to strike me, but they didn't do it, and if they had I don't know what I should have done ; but God made a way of escape, somehow or other, so they didn't strike me.

Now, I want you all to take hold here to-night, and make this an interesting meeting. You can't find any better place than this to go. Just hear this singing. Talk about your paid choirs, why this beats them all ! Some of

them get their ten thousand dollars a year, but they can't
compare with this. I have a great many gentlemen and
ladies, uptown and down, speak to me about this wonderful singing, and they all say they never heard the like. Do
you know why? because we're singing for Jesus here!
That's what makes the melody, "making melody in your
hearts!" Now, let all speak, and tell what God has done for
your souls.

*   *   *   *   *   *

I am a monument to God's grace and God's mercy and
God's forbearance. The longer I live the more I see it and
feel it. May the Lord keep me humble! May the Lord
keep me grateful! I don't care much about the world; it
looks small to me. Perhaps it would look bigger if I had
better health. I have cause to love God. He picked me
up from a terrible hole, and washed me from my sins.
Now you have heard the biggest debtor to grace that is in
the room; let the next heaviest debtor follow me.

HUMBLE AND HAPPY.

The Lord has been at work, and the more the Lord
works the more humble I feel. I pray God to keep me so,
for I know that without Him I could do nothing. I have
nothing to be proud of; I am proud of my Saviour, and not
of myself. I was a notorious drunkard and gambler. Even
my wife does not know some of the sins I committed, and
she never will till the Day of Judgment. I don't know
what to say to express my feelings of thankfulness. I
know I have been converted, that is, if conversion is
ceasing to love that which is evil and loving that which is
good. I know that divine grace saved me from a drunk-

ard's grave. Now there are many here who can thank God with me for saving them, and whom he has cleaned inside and out. They ought to tell others the story. Don't let us be like the nine lepers who were healed by the Lord Jesus, and never came back to thank Him.

HE HAD GOT RELIGION.

I don't encourage any one to be careless or to run any risk of falling from God, but when they *do* fall I shall take them back again and help them to God. It is a dangerous thing to give way to sin and fall from our love to God! We might fall *once too often* and die ere we could recover. Yes, it's dangerous to fall even *once*, for God might cut us off. Oh, how terrible it would be! Why it's like stepping right out of heaven into hell! Isn't it awful? I fell three times when I first started. I was ignorant; I knew nothing of the Christian life or its peculiar duties or perils, so I had to learn by bitter experience. Some persons have asked me, " Do you really believe you were converted before your falls?" Yes, I was; I know I was converted while in a prison-cell. Why, I was so happy I fell like a dead man on my cell-floor, and didn't know anything for a long while. When I got up I couldn't contain myself. I knocked things around and shouted, and I suppose made a terrible to-do. The keeper heard it,—a tall old Jew we called " Shadpole," because he was so long and slim,—and slipping along with his slippered feet to my door he peeked in between the bars and hollered, half-scared like, " What's the matter in there?" I didn't answer him, but kept right on; I couldn't help it; and he yelled again:

" Say, what's the matter?"

" Oh," I cried, " I've got religion !"

" What ?"

" I've got r-e-l-i-g-i-o-n," I answered again.

"I'll give you r-e-l-i-g-i-o-n," he growled, and proceeded to take down my number for a cold shower-bath for next morning. I suppose he thought I needed cooling off, *but I never got it.* The Lord made that man lose his book or get confused about the number or something, for I was not punished at all. I went to work after that conversion like any other converted man, and if I do say it myself, others were led to God. I only had a half hour at a time, but I improved it among my fellow-prisoners to say a word of kindness, and we would often shed tears together. Oh yes, I believe I was converted even though I was so foolish as to fall away for a season afterwards. I believe you may possibly fall away, but I advise you to come back quickly, get forgiven, and never run any risk of falling again by your own carelessness or failure to watch and pray, and trust Jesus. I never could see how any Christian could be idle. I can't keep still ; I must be doing something for others, or I'd die.

THOUGHT HE WOULD BE A DETECTIVE.

Did you ever hear how near I came to being a regular paid detective? Well, I'll tell you. I thought I might as well do something for myself, and concluding I'd make a good detective I went to A. T. Stewart's large place and applied for a position as a detective. The man looked at me awhile and seemed dubious about it.

"Don't you know," he asked, " that it requires a great deal of talent to be a detective?"

The People of the State of New York,

To all to whom these Presents shall Come:

Whereas, At a Court held in and for our County of _New York_ _____ in the month of _January_ 1857, _Jeremiah McCauley_ _____ and was thereupon sentenced to be imprisoned in the State Prison at _Sing Sing_ at hard labor, for _the term of fifteen years six months;_ and he being represented unto us as worthy of being restored to the rights of a citizen:

Therefore, Know Ye, That we have pardoned, reprised, and released, and by these Presents do pardon, remiso and release the said _Jeremiah McCauley_ of and from the offence whereof in our said Court he stands convicted as aforesaid, and of and from all Sentences, Judgments and Executions thereupon, and he is hereby restored to all the rights of a citizen.

In Testimony Whereof, We have caused these our Letters to be made Patent, and the Great Seal of our said State to be hereunto affixed.

Witness, John A. Dix, Governor of our said State, at our city of Albany, the _Second_ day of _October_ in the year of our Lord one thousand eight hundred and seventy-three.

John A. Dix

PASSED THE SECRETARY'S OFFICE, THE
2d DAY OF _October_ 1873.

Diss Bixoll
SECRETARY OF STATE

"Yes, I know it, and I believe I have the necessary talent, sir, to make a success of it."

"Have you had any previous experience in this work, and knowledge of the class of characters you will have to deal with?"

"Oh, yes, quite an experience."

"Where, and under what circumstances?"

So I had to tell him who I was, what I'd been, and all about it. When I got through he looked at me in astonishment for a moment, but finally said, "You will undoubtedly hear from me in a few days in regard to this matter. I'll send you our decision in that time. I can encourage you with the assurance that it will be favorable to your wishes."

I went home, and was looking for the man to send me the answer, but before he had time to do so the Lord sent me the pneumonia and laid me upon my back for six weeks; so my detective job was all lost, and I've stuck to the mission work. God has given me a great many souls for which I am very grateful, and am very much encouraged to hold on as long as I may live.

LAST TESTIMONIES.

It was Jerry McAuley's earnest desire to testify with his dying breath to the power of saving grace. This God permitted him to do publicly up to within a very few days of his departure. On the evening of Friday, September 12, less than a week before his death, he said in the Mission meeting:

"I feel as if I want to testify always, and even with my *dying breath*, to the goodness of God in saving me. Sometimes I do not seem to have words to express my feelings

of thankfulness to Him for His great mercy, or words to
praise Him for His goodness in saving me from going down
to perdition."

On the night of Sunday, September 14, his last Sunday on
earth, after listening to the story of the woman of Samaria,
Jerry said: "She was a hard case. Respectable women
would not have associated with her; but the Son of God
condescended to talk with her." Our brother spoke of the
woman's selfishness. She wanted Christ's gift so that she
might not any longer have the trouble of coming to the
well to draw water. He then spoke of himself as he once
was, in no mild or measured terms. "I was a brute, I was
one of the worst devils ever let loose in society, but the
glorious Gospel contained in that blessed Bible civilized me.
It is the greatest civilizer in the world. There is no power
like it. It made a man and a Christian and a good citizen
of me."

CHAPTER XII.

CALLED HOME.

"My kingly King at His right hand
My presence doth command,
Where glory, glory dwelleth,
In Immanuel's land."

IN the dealings of God with his people infinite wisdom and infinite love ever blend. All things, death included, work together for good to those who love the Lord. Thus while we record the decease of him to whose memory these pages are devoted, it is in the blessed confidence that there was no mistake in the time of his departure. Our God knew best when to take his servant. Jerry McAuley was called home on September 18, 1884, being then forty-five years of age. He had long been ailing, and knew that the call home would probably come suddenly when it did come. And sudden indeed it was! On the day previous to his death Jerry was in the very best of spirits. In the afternoon he and Mrs. McAuley spent a brief while in Central Park, but immediately on their return home Jerry was seized with a hemorrhage of the lungs. Physicians were sent for and speedily arrived. It was on that night, while expecting that every moment would be his last, that he said to one of the converts of the Mission, pointing upward as he spoke, "It's all right up there." He was too much exhausted to say more. Soon there came a little relief and some promise of improvement. On the morning of Thursday he requested his wife to read a psalm to him, and he listened with evident interest as she did so. On Thursday afternoon, when his wife said to him, " Jesus is your Saviour," he twice nodded assent. At four o'clock, or a very few minutes after, another hemorrhage came on, and within three minutes his spirit had taken its flight. Pain and suffering were for him things of the past. He had entered into his reward.

Since Jesus wept at the grave of Lazarus, it cannot be wrong for us to weep in the hour of bereavement; but while we sorrow, we do " not sorrow as those who have no hope." The Christian sings,

> " Death no longer now we die;
> We but follow Christ on high."

The loss of a friend, the loss of an honest, loving, consecrated worker we mourn. Yet, with resigned hearts and submissive wills, we bow to the dispensation of our all-wise and ever-loving Father in Heaven, and say, " Even so, Father; for so it seemed good in Thy sight." Remembering how God saved Jerry McAuley, and how useful in winning souls God made him, we rather rejoice at the sanctified life and its glorious success, than mourn at the so-called death. Nay, as we think of the reward that awaited him, the rest that remained for him, the welcome of the Redeemer, the greeting of many now in glory who were saved through his instrumentality, we can even rejoice at his departure.

Even his death was not without fruit. One who looked upon his face as the body lay in the casket, then and there resolved by God's help to start in the new life. Nor has Jerry ceased to serve the Lord whom he loved. In that bright world where he now is the inhabitants serve their King unceasingly. They rest not day nor night doing his will. Saved from a life of sin, let us thank God that Jerry McAuley was TRANSFORMED; saved forever from suffering and sorrow, let us thank God that he has been TRANSLATED.

The following account of the Memorial Service held in the Broadway Tabernacle is taken from *Jerry McAuley's Newspaper*, of which mention has already been made. The account of the Memorial Service at No. 316 Water Street is from the same source.

Broadway Tabernacle, Thirty-fourth Street and Sixth Avenue, was thronged on Sunday afternoon last (Sept. 21). The audience-room, the long deep galleries, the many aisles, the doorways and vestibules, were crowded. Hundrens of disappointed people were unable to find entrance, and turned away, many of them after coming miles to be present at the Memorial Service. The exercises commenced at half-past two o'clock. The Rev. S. Irenæus Prime, D.D., senior editor of the *New York Observer*, presided. The Tabernacle choir sang some pieces, and Mr. George W. Stebbins sang some solos.

It was a most solemn and affecting service. The Rev. Dr. Deems, Pastor of the Church of the Strangers, read the Scriptures, and when he came to the words, "Forasmuch as ye know that your labor is not in vain in the Lord," our hearts felt that this was peculiarly true of Jerry McAuley's work.

Dr. Prime, before calling upon the speakers who had

been chosen to address the large audience, referred briefly
to his intimate acquaintance with the deceased. In him,
he said, we had proof that the grace proclaimed in our holy
religion could save and keep any man. If that could not,
nothing could.

The Rev. Dr. William M. Taylor, Pastor of the Broadway Tabernacle Church, had just returned from Europe.
The second item of intelligence he received on his return
was the fact of Jerry McAuley's death. He had thought
of the words of St. Paul, "As sorrowing, yet always rejoicing." To the widow it brought sorrow, and there was
sorrow as we thought of the loss sustained in the work.
But to both sorrows there was a sure antidote.

"We commend the widow," he said, "to the Saviour. He
will minister to her comfort, until the call shall come to
her, ' Come up higher.'

"In thinking of the man and his work, there are one or
two things which have been deeply impressed upon my
mind. As I have listened to his testimony, and the
testimonies of those whom he has led to Christ, I have
said, 'I am not ashamed of the Gospel of Christ, for *it is*
the power of God unto salvation to them that believe.' If
Jerry could be saved, who not? After Jerry, anybody!
The world's outcasts can be saved by Christ. Jerry would
say, and he could say it without affectation, ' Christ Jesus
came into the world to save sinners, and I am chief.'
Jerry was an instance of a conversion in prison. We sometimes get an idea that there is no use in sending chaplains
to prisons. There is a good deal of a feeling of despair in
the Church about work for prisoners. We should have
greater faith in such work. Let us learn to think more

for them when coming out of prison. Just as Paul in Damascus fell into the hands of Barnabas, Jerry at length fell into good hands. He once said he felt it so good to be trusted after he came out of prison.

"'Deal gently with the erring, as thy God hath dealt with thee!' Jerry's case is a beautiful illustration of how God brings good out of evil. Through the evil of Jerry's early life God fitted him for special labor. A history like that helps one to understand what God means when He says, 'I will restore the years which the locusts have eaten.' The years destroyed by sin were made up by the multiplied usefulness of the later years of Jerry's life. Thus let sinners put themselves in the Lord's hands. He will restore the years which the locusts have eaten. What a glorious Gospel! What a powerful Saviour! What a wonderful Redeemer we have! Haply some one is here to-day, almost swept in by the crowd, who is enslaved by evil habits. Take courage. As contact with the bones of the prophet Elisha started the dead man into life, so coming into contact with the truths this casket preaches now may you be brought to life!"

Mr. A. S. Hatch, Jerry McAuley's old and tried friend, spoke with great feeling. "The impulses of my heart," he said, "would lead me to sit beside this casket a silent mourner; but," he added, "no one except his wife knew Jerry better than I did. It was my privilege in the beginning of his struggle up toward a better life to encourage him by the warm grasp of a helping hand and to speak to him words of hope and cheer; and it has been my privilege also, when clouds and darkness have gathered about my own pathway, to be uplifted and comforted by the simple and childlike, yet robust faith of Jerry and his wife, and by their sublime trust in the loving Providence of God.   If I should keep silence I might seem faithless to the memory of my dead friend.

" Jerry McAuley is dead.   There are but few names which linked with such an announcement would have aroused a more widespread interest than is felt to-day wherever men say to each other ' Jerry is dead;' not because a great man, as the world counts greatness, is gone, but in recognition of a humble, sincere, and earnest life, devoted for sixteen years to the uplifting and saving of lost men and women.   The flags of the city are not at half-mast to-day; no drums will beat in the funeral procession that will bear him to his last resting-place to-morrow; no volleys will be fired over his grave.   Yet thousands of lowly hearts are bowed down with grief for the friend they have lost; while men and women in all classes of life who owe him a debt of gratitude they are not ashamed to own, are pondering with bowed heads and chastened hearts the lessons of the life and death of this once despised and hunted river thief, but for sixteen years the chosen servant of God, signally honored and used of Him.   No fulsome eulogy would be in place over this now still and lifeless form.   Could Jerry rise up in his coffin and speak, he would himself rebuke the man who should utter it.   For Jerry gloried not in himself, but in the blessed Saviour who had transformed him from what he once had been to what by wondrous grace he had become.   He was always humble, for he always remembered the pit from which he had been digged.   He continually rejoiced in the power of Divine love, and of the grace of Jesus Christ that could so save and keep such as he.   He used to say to the outcasts who felt that they were so low down in sin that there was no hope and no salvation for them, 'There is hope in Jesus Christ for *anybody*, for He saved *me*.' His labors spent for the salvation and redemption of the lost were not in vain ; and his steadfastness to the end, and his triumphant death, have now confirmed and empha- sized the lessons of his life, and his constantly reiterated testimony to the power of Jesus to save. The Church of Christ needed the lesson of his sixteen years of labor, and their wonderful fruits. Although theoretically all Christians believe that the vilest sinner may be saved, yet there is much practical unbelief and scepticism on the subject, when they are brought face to face with some of the worst forms of human depravity and of the wretchedness wrought by sin, and are called upon to believe, and to act as if they believed in reality, that individual human wrecks are worth trying to save. It is this lesson, that none are so utterly lost but there is hope in laboring for their salvation, that there is no depth of human degradation to which the arm of Jesus cannot reach down and from which His grace cannot lift the sinner up, that the life and work of Jerry have taught us. In conclusion, I would hold up Jerry, as he loved best to hold himself up, as I know he would most wish to be held up in this place to-day—as a monument of divine grace, as a signal example of the power of Jesus' blood to cleanse the vilest sinner.

" Let our lives be such that when we are called upon to step out from the ranks of the living and take our places in the shadowy procession of the dead, we may be able, as Jerry was, to look back upon years spent in earnest work for the Master, and looking forward and upward say with Jerry, 'It's all right.' "

Mr. Sidney Whittemore then spoke of the world-wide

influence of the deceased's work. Many had gone out from Water Street to be missionaries all over the globe. Jerry was strong as a lion for courage, yet had a heart gentle as a woman's. He once spoke roughly to a man who refused to cease his musical performances during the hours of the Mission services, and afterwards went to the man to ask his forgiveness for his somewhat hasty words—and this although the man's insults had brought them out.

The Rev. Dr. Deems said a stranger might well ask the meaning of this great audience. 'Here were the clergy, here were men of means, women of culture, all come to pay a tribute of respect to whom? To a hunted river-thief. It was the romance of grace and of Providence. It was not his ancestry, his beauty, his brains, or his services to science that brought out these thousands of people. It was all because one day in prison Jerry accepted God's offer of salvation, and took Christ as his present, personal, and sufficient Saviour then and there. We could all do that. Then he was a forcible illustration of the possibility of the redemption of a human soul from the bottomless pit of the lowest degradation. Why labor with such—they will fall back? many asked, but here was one man who for sixteen years had fought the battle against the old sins and lusts and passions, and had conquered. Dr. Deems closed with an eloquent appeal to the unsaved. Were there not some present who had heard Jerry's appeals from the Mission platform and who had not heeded them. Though Jerry's uttered appeals had not moved them, should not the appeal of his silent lips win them now?

These addresses were followed by the singing of a solo by Mr. Stebbins, who rendered it with his usual tender pathos amid the intense silence of the audience. As he sung the words,

> " We too must come to the river side,
>   One by one, one by one ;
>   We're nearer its brink each evening tide,
>   One by one, one by one,"

the stillness seemed almost painful, and it was difficult to restrain the pent-up feelings of the heart. The Rev. Wilbur F. Watkins followed in a prayer that was most tender and touching : the choir sang " I will sing of my Redeemer," and Dr. Prime invoked the apostolic benediction.

The casket containing the remains of the deceased was decorated with floral tributes at once chaste and beautiful. A cross lay thereupon, and at the close of the prayer offered by Dr. Watkins the rays of sunlight which had been streaming through the windows all the afternoon reached the cross, and by their effulgence lit it up with a dazzling brightness. It seemed as though Heaven would bear shining witness to the efficacy of the cross as the power by which our departed brother had been lifted out of darkness into light, out of death into life. It was a most impressive incident and a striking type. The light of God's saving power does fall on the cross of Calvary, and at the cross is light, the light of hope and life for all, no matter how lowly nor how lost.

The service over, the audience passed by the coffin to take a farewell look at the remains of the honored missionary, nearly two hours being occupied by the sorrowing throng in paying this tribute of respect to the dead. Next day all that was mortal of the deceased was laid away in Woodlawn Cemetery. There the sacred dust will rest until the archangel's trump shall sound, and those who have fallen asleep in Christ shall rise immortal. "Precious in the sight of the Lord is the death of his saints" (Psalm cxvi. 15). "Blessed are the dead which die in the Lord from henceforth. Yea, saith the Spirit, that they may rest from their labors; and their works do follow them" (Rev. xiv. 13).

> "There is no death! The stars go down,
> To rise upon some fairer shore;
> And bright in heaven's jewelled crown
> They shine for evermore."

The following incident, published in the New York *Herald* at the time of Jerry's funeral, serves to show how ready Jerry was with a word of sympathy for any one in trouble who came across his path. It shows also that such words are remembered and treasured even by those whose appearance promises little lasting impression.

Two gentlemen—one of them a representative of the *Herald*—were standing at or near one of the entrances of the Tabernacle, when a shabby-looking old man, who had been lounging on the outskirts of the crowd, approached them and said:

"'Beg pardin, gents, but seein' as you were kinnected here and seein' as how I ain't posted on ways and things, I thought I'd ask you for a favor.'

"Both of the listeners were turning away expecting an untimely appeal for alms. But the other said, 'I've heard it's the right thing to send flowers and sich to put on the coffin of any one who's bin good to you. Well, I don't know, gents, whether I've got the rights of it or not. But there's somethin' here for Jerry.'

"He took off his tall, battered hat as he spoke, and felt in it with trembling fingers. 'It ain't any great shakes,' he said, and he took out a little bunch of white flowers. Then looking up, as though to read in the faces of the listeners approval or disapproval, he went on, apologetically : 'They're no great shakes, I allow, and I 'spect they mayn't set off the roses and things rich people send. I'm a poor man, you know, but when I heard Jerry was gone, I gets up and says to myself, "Go on and do what's fash'nable ; that's the way folks do when they want to show a dead man's done a heap for 'em." So there they are.'

"The usher took them.

"'And when you drop 'em with the rest, though they ain't no great shakes,' he added, with the old apologetic look, 'Jerry, who was my friend, 'll know,' and his voice trembled ; 'he'll know they come from old Joe Chappy.'

"'What did he do for you?' the reporter ventured.

"'A great deal,' the old man replied. 'But it's long ago now. My gal had gone to the bad, and was dyin' without ever a bite for her to eat. I got around drunk, but it sobered me, and I hustled about to hunt up some good man. N. G. They asked if she went to Sunday-school and all that. O' course she didn't. How cud the poor gal? Well, they called her names, sed she wus a child o' wrath, and I went away broken-hearted, when I come across Jerry, and he went home with me and comforted me, and he sed that Almighty God wouldn't be rough on a poor gal what didn't know no better. She died then, but I ain't forgot Jerry.'

"The poor old wreck could not be prevailed upon to enter, and the crowd was so great that the little bunch of flowers could not reach the casket. But the reporter thought, as he saw the floral emblems there, that none of them would be sweeter to the dead than that simple offering."

The incident is a true one, and the little bunch of white flowers has been tenderly preserved by Mrs. McAuley. Who shall say that the memory of Jerry and of some further word spoken by him may not be the means even yet of bringing the man who gave them to a knowledge of Jerry's Saviour?

CHAPTER XIII.

ON THE OLD SPOT.

"The dead are like the stars by day,
Withdrawn from mortal eye,
Yet holding unperceived their way
Through the unclouded sky.

"By them, through holy hope and love,
We feel, in hours serene,
Connected with a world above,
Immortal and unseen."

THE Memorial Meeting held at 316 Water Street on Sunday afternoon, September 28, will not be forgotten by those who were present. Not only were tributes of esteem to the memory of Jerry McAuley uttered by those who were coworkers with him or who knew him and his work, but many who had been led by him to Christ testified as to what grace had done for them through our departed brother.

It was eminently appropriate to hold a memorial service on the old spot where he commenced his work, and where for so many years God so richly blessed him to the salvation of souls. The Mission-hall was packed, and at every window were persons who could not find room inside, but bore the discomfort of standing all the way through, listening with deepest attention.

The exercises commenced precisely at the hour arranged, half-past two, and continued for two full hours with unflag-

10

ging interest. General Clinton B. Fisk presided, and after
the congregation had sung the hymn, "They are gathering
homeward one by one," called on Rev. J. W. Sanford to
read from the Bible and pray. The Scriptures selected were
most appropriate, and were impressively read, the prayer
was simple and solemn, and then we sang the words, " I
heard the Saviour say, etc." The chorus brought to General Fisk's recollection some of the scenes in the old Mission
building, which preceded the one in which we met on this
Sabbath afternoon. Often in the old days, when, kneeling
with Jerry and his wife and others, some soul was born into
the Kingdom, Jerry would say, "sing ' Jesus paid it all.' "
Reference was made to the memorial meeting of the previous Sabbath at Broadway Tabernacle. The audience on
that occasion the speaker likened to a slice of metropolitan
life cut lengthways, so that there was some of the top crust,
some of the bottom crust, and some of all between. The
best of saints and the most sinful of all were there. Men
high in financial circles, in social life, and in professional life,
were the pall-bearers in the funeral procession which wended
its way from 104 West Thirty-second Street to the Tabernacle. A stranger might have asked, Who is this at whose
death the city is stirred? Was he a great warrior whose
sword saved the Republic? No! although he was a victor,
his victories were those of mercy, not of carnage. He
was not a statesman eminent in the forum. He was a simple, unlettered man. On his coffin were the words, " Died
September 18, 1884. Jeremiah McAuley, aged 45 years."
That was the story.

He had been one of the worst of men, but became one
of the best, simply through the blood of the Lord Jesus
Christ. Accepting Christ for himself, he had been used

of God to preach the Gospel by his words and by his walk.

General Fisk spoke of his early association with Jerry in the work, and of its extended influence. In Liverpool one night he heard a rough-looking sailor speak in a seamen's mission-meeting. Though the man was rough his face shone. "I found Jesus over there in America," he said, and all who heard him listened in wonder. This man was known as Swearing Johnny. "When we were paid off I took my money to the saloons, and then pretty soon I was drunk again. Then I went out into the street, and the snow was beating against my face. As I passed along the street I heard singing, and stopped to listen. I heard them sing 'Jesus loves even me.' 'I'll go in and see about it,' I said to myself." He went in and there he saw "that wonderful man, Jerry McAuley," and *he* led him to Christ. "Yes," said his wife, "and it has been nothing but Jerry McAuley and 'Jesus loves even me' ever since Johnny's ship came home." At Marseilles General Fisk heard a very similar testimony from another redeemed man, and Mrs. McAuley, he said, had letters from all parts of the globe—letters baptized with many tears—which testified to the work done by this one good man. The speaker concluded with an earnest appeal for renewed consecration. "Let us consecrate ourselves anew to the service," he said. "Catch the standard ere it falls. In the first regiment I led into the field in the war, the boy who carried the banner fell almost at the first firing; his brother sprang forward and grasped the standard, so that our flag never went down. See that the standard that Jerry has dropped be not allowed to fall."

One of the early and most helpful friends of the deceased

missionary was the Hon. William E. Dodge, now in glory. He was often in the Mission meeting, and knelt with those who sought salvation and prayed and labored with them. The memory of his love of the work made it all the more pleasant to hear from his son, the Rev. E. Stuart Dodge. He likened Jerry to a jewel taken up from the depths, but the speaker would have us glory not in Jerry McAuley but in the grace magnified in him. We must remember in speaking of him that he always glorified his Master. He told men and women that Jesus could save. Poor lost souls came to him and heard that there was a Saviour mighty to save, and so were converted. Jerry honored the Gospel as revealed in the Bible. He read the Bible, talked the Bible, preached the Bible. It was God's Word, and in it was revealed the power of God to save. Jerry believed in prayer. When he prayed he did not pray all around the universe. If he was interested in a soul he just prayed for that particular soul, and God heard and saved. Moreover, Jerry believed in hand-picked souls. The best fruit is not shaken from the tree, but picked by hand, one by one. So he would hold up Christ before one soul. He believed in the power of the Spirit of God. He did not believe that his efforts or anybody's else would save. He believed that God's Spirit would bless the truth about the blood so that it would do its own convicting and converting work. "What a difference this truth worked in him! Once a dock thief, Jerry McAuley went up to heaven, his arms all full of sheaves. Let us magnify and honor the Gospel of God, which makes such a change!" Two thoughts the speaker impressed in closing. "If there is one here who has not given his heart to the Saviour," he said, "remember that God saved Jerry McAuley, and He can save you. God lifted Jerry up, and you have no right, therefore, to despair or to doubt God's mercy. Christian workers, since God used this instrument for His own mighty purposes, no one can say, 'God cannot use me.' We cannot do Jerry McAuley's work, but we can do our work as Jerry did his— with consecrated hearts and true faith."

Rev. E. D. Murphy was the next speaker. He has been pastor of the Mariners' Church on Catherine Street for more than twenty years. He said that thinking of what Water Street was twenty years ago, this audience seemed perfectly wonderful. It was at that time one of the worst streets in the city. He recollected the first religious meeting attempted there. He recalled, too, the first time that he ever saw Jerry McAuley. The latter was rather a rough-looking man then. It was in the midst of the John Allen excitement that Jerry came to him and said, " I've served the devil very faithfully in the Fourth Ward " (the Bloody Fourth, it was often called then), " and now I want to try to do something for the people there. If some person would rent a building, I would fit it for men who have just come out of State's Prison." He would have cots for them to sleep on, and bread and coffee to give them in the morning, he said, and have a prayer-meeting for them in the evening. Mr. Murphy had no doubt of Jerry's honesty, sincerity, and earnestness; but he must confess that he did doubt the man's ability and judgment. Not liking to discourage him, he recommended him to see Mr. A. S. Hatch, and Rev. G. J. Mingins, the city missionary in that ward. The next thing Dr. Murphy heard about it was that a building had been rented and the work was begun. " We learn that God's ways are not our ways," said the speaker " Who would ever have thought of selecting Jerry for the

work he did.   But Jesus died to save sinners, and in His
sight a thief's soul is as precious as any.   God desired to
reach such, and so made choice of one of the least promising, and baptized him and filled him with the Holy Ghost,
and told him to go to work."   Jerry's ready mother-wit,
the tenderness of his appeals to the unsaved, his prayers, so
simple, tender, gentle, as though talking with the Lord, and
his personal work with souls, passed under review.   Then
Dr. Murphy said that hundreds of sailors had come under
his notice in his church work, who had been led to Christ
by Jerry McAuley.   Every single night Jerry had hold of
somebody.

Dr. Murphy concluded his remarks by emphasizing the
value of personal work with souls.   In connection with his
house of worship are eight or nine inquiry-rooms which
have proved the birthplace of many souls.   In personal conversation men cannot pass the truth presented over to their
neighbors.   They know it is addressed to them individually.
At the close of the address two of the members of Dr.
Murphy's choir sang a duet :

> " We shall sleep, but not forever,
> There awaits a glorious dawn,
> We shall meet to part—no never, etc."

General Fisk said he had letters from some of the Cremorne Mission trustees, expressing regret at their inability
to attend the service, owing to absence from town.   Messrs.
J. Noble Stearns, John H. Boswell, Samuel E. Hiscox, and
James Talcott were all heard from.   The latter closed with
these words : "As we hold this service in his memory, may
our own hearts be filled with a deeper love for Christ, and
our lives receive a fresh impulse to work for souls, that the

world shall not be poorer because this brave, true heart has gone to its reward."

Mr. A. S. Hatch, another of the trustees, and who was used under God as a sheet-anchor for Jerry McAuley when the latter started on his career as a Christian worker, followed with an address. The chairman said that Jerry would often speak to him of Mr. Hatch's good help. " I could not have struggled on to success," the redeemed man would say, " had it not been for the brotherly sympathy and helpfulness that Christ Jesus inspired toward me in the heart of Mr. Hatch. He trusted me, General, and that's what saved me."

Mr. Hatch said that he loved Jerry with a love and sorrowed for him with a sorrow which could not be expressed in words, and he would not therefore attempt to speak of his own emotions at his death. But here on the spot where Jerry first bore testimony to the power of the Lord Jesus to save, and where he first commenced his work, the speaker thought it peculiarly fitting to draw some lessons from his life. He was a remarkable man in many respects. Almost without worldly education he became by grace and prayer and the study of God's Word learned in the wisdom that is from above. He had a remarkably vivid apprehension of those portions of Scripture which are particularly adapted to the class whom he mainly sought to reach. Those who had heard him speak of the prodigal son, of the thief on the cross, of the publican in the temple, of the woman taken in adultery, or of her who washed the feet of Jesus with her tears and wiped them with the hairs of her head, would never forget it. The sweetness and tenderness which grace had infused into that naturally rough nature were wonderful to see, and would ever be remembered by those who

had seen them poured out over kneeling and repentant
sinners, or experienced them in private relations of personal
friendship. It was beautiful to see the flowers and fruits
of grace blossoming and ripening on the branches which
Jesus had grafted on that rugged trunk. A more earnest,
faithful, conscientious, and devoted laborer for the Master
whom he loved, and for the lost men and women over whom
his heart yearned, never lived than Jerry McAuley. Jerry
loved to proclaim the power of Jesus to save to the uttermost all who come to God by him. It was not two weeks
since the speaker was asked if he believed there were any
permanent results from this mission work. " Why, look at
Jerry," was the reply; "he has stood." " Well, perhaps
he'll slip," was the inquirer's response. When Mr. Hatch
told Mrs. McAuley of this incident a day or two previously,
she replied, "Yes, he has slipped—slipped into heaven."
The speaker said that the truth proclaimed by Jerry so constantly in his life, namely, Christ's power to save to the uttermost, had been enforced and emphasized by Jerry's
death. His steadfastness to the end and his triumphant
death had silenced forever the doubting suggestion that
he might yet fall away. He could not fall now. Another
lesson learned was that it paid to work for, and spend
time and money for the redemption of, the outcast and degraded. It was worth while to spend time and money on
any soul for whom Christ had died.

In concluding Mr. Hatch said that to the unsaved sinner,
despairing perhaps because so low down in sin that he thinks
there is no salvation for him, Jerry seemed to be saying
still, " Look at me! Jesus saved me : there is hope for you."
To the child of God he said that no labor, money, or pains
spent in proclaiming the Gospel to the lost and perishing is

spent in vain. If Jerry's death should enforce these lessons, he would not have died in vain.

The order of the meeting was then changed. The appointed speakers had accomplished their tasks, and those who owed their conversion to Jerry McAuley, as God's chosen instrument in connection with his Water Street work, were asked to speak. Mr. J. F. Shorey, the superintendent of the Water Street Mission, said he was saved in connection with Messrs. Moody and Sankey's meetings in New York, eight years ago. He had not long been intimately acquainted with Jerry personally, but he had become very familiar with the results of his work, as he had heard so many testify how Jerry had led them to Christ.

Several converts followed, and their testimonies were most touching, full of expressions of gratitude to God for having brought them under Jerry's influence.

Of one of these tributes of gratitude—first to God, and then to Jerry—a full report was kept. It was the tribute of a young man. He said :

" It was eight years ago last February that I came from my home in Brooklyn to the Water Street Mission. I had never heard testimonies before, but then I heard young men saying how happy they had been since Jesus saved them. I thought that if he saved them he would save me. I had a good home and Christian parents, but I was not happy, for I was sinning against God. Jerry got hold of me, and bid me go up to the bench, and the friends would pray for me. Well, I determined to put my trust in God's promises, and that night I started in the new way. Next night I went to the Mission again. I had not had a good day. I had not acted as a Christian ; so when Jerry asked me, 'How do you feel to-day ; how have you got

along?' I told him it had been a pretty poor day with me.
'Well, don't be discouraged,' he replied, and then bid me
go again to the bench and pray. I had a happier day next
day. In the evening Jerry said to me, 'Well, how has it
been to-day?' Then when I told him that I had been
happier and had felt Christ's keeping power, he responded,
'Get up and tell us about it then.' This was eight years
ago, and Jesus saves me to-day. One night I remember
that some sailors were at the bench—*that dear old bench*—
where so many found the Saviour. We almost reverenced
it! One of these sailors longed to trust the Saviour, but
could not see the way clear. How could he trust so as to
be kept safe henceforth? That was the question. Said
Jerry, 'Can't you trust the Lord from here to the door?'
Yes, he thought he could do that. 'Then can't you trust
Him from the door to the corner?' was the next question.
Light burst into the man's heart and beamed upon his face,
and he exclaimed, 'I see the whole of it, glory to God.' It
is just trusting Jesus, simply trusting every day. I have
not only Christian parents now, but I have a Christian wife
too. I owe my salvation and all the blessing that has
come since under God to Jerry McAuley. I put the Lord
Jesus first and Jerry McAuley after. When men used to
talk of what Jerry had done for them, he would say, 'Don't
give me any glory, boys; give God the glory. If I have
been of any use to you it is all God working through me.'
In Jerry's death I have lost one of my best friends."

Could any words have more forcibly shown first Jerry's
humility, and next his apt way of dealing with souls? He
encouraged new converts in the early days of their Christian
life; when they felt that they had made any progress and
overcome any temptation through Christ, he would have

them rise and testify. The testimony helped and strengthened the converts who uttered it ; encouraged other converts, and impressed those who were yet in the darkness
and bondage of sin. How suggestive, too, the words,
"Don't give me any glory, boys!" To be successful in
Christian work, self must be kept down, and Christ must be
exalted. In Water Street, at the Cremorne Mission, any-
where, everywhere, God honors those who seek to honor
and glorify Him.

CHAPTER XIV.

CHARACTERISTIC SKETCHES AND PERSONAL RECOLLECTIONS OF JERRY McAULEY.

By A. S. Hatch.

The ways of God are oft beyond our ken,
And wiser far than ways of mortal men;
Whom man rejects, the Lord doth often use;
His corner-stone the builders did refuse.

I became acquainted with Jerry McAuley about the time of his restoration from the sad relapse into which he had fallen after his release from Sing Sing prison. The desperate and reckless life which he had led in the interval, as bounty-broker, gambler, prize-fighter, rough, drunkard, and river-thief, is graphically portrayed in his autobiography.

All this, with his previous criminal and prison life, had left an unmistakable impress upon him, and his appearance told plainly enough what he had been.

To the ordinary observer he was perhaps as hard and hopeless a looking case as one would be likely to encounter in tramping the worst streets of New York day and night for a month; and in his dull eye, rough aspect, and illiterate speech, there was little promise of the future evangelist, or of the wonderful career of consecrated usefulness in the salvation of depraved and outcast men and women and of Christian influence, reaching to all classes in life, which has since made his name familiar, and his life and work a sacred memory, among those who love Jesus and believe in His power to save. It would have been a penetrating eye and a lively faith indeed that could at that time have transfigured Jerry, in imagination, into an instrument of moral and religious force in the world, even in the hands of Divine power.

It is with no irreverent memory of my dead friend that I sketch this picture of him as he then appeared. It is only a dim reflection of the portrait which, with inimitable effect of mingled pathos and drollery, he used to paint of himself as he was when the missionary found him in his den in Cherry Street; not that he gloried in the picture, or in the revelations of sin and crime of which it was the product, but because he gloried in the power of Jesus to save, and loved to magnify that power, and to illustrate it by what was to him its most real and conscious manifestation—the contrast between what sin had once made him, and that to which grace had redeemed him.

Shortly before the time of which I am writing, Mr. Oliver Dyer, a vigorous writer on current local events, had written and published in *Packard's Monthly* for July, 1868, an article entitled "The Wickedest Man in New York," which had a wide circulation and excited a profound interest. It was extensively reproduced in the daily and weekly papers throughout the country, and eagerly read by all classes. It was a revelation to many of the moral and Christian people of New York and elsewhere, who had before known nothing of the inner life of the dance-houses, rat-pits, and other centres of vice and human degradation with which Water Street and its surrounding thoroughfares were at that time crowded. It brought down on that previously benighted region an army of curiosity-seekers, clergymen, missionaries, religious enthusiasts, and others, who contemplated the scene of the "Wickedest Man's" exploits with varied emotions and comments. Some good people were distressed with the thought that Oliver Dyer had only succeeded in advertising the dreadful business on which the locality thrived, and, by investing it with a spice of romance, had only made its naked repulsiveness more alluring to the vicious tastes of many who had previously shunned it as too deep a depth for them. But the keen wits of the proprietors of the dens which filled the neighborhood, and their practical eye to financial results, soon grasped the true outcome of it all; and they hit the nail on the head when they said with blunt sincerity, "It has spoiled our business. All these white cho-kers and black coats, and all this respectability, and hymn-singin', and prayin', and preachin', are keeping away our customers; and these fellows don't buy any beer or whiskey, or dance with the girls." And after a few months many of them had thrown up the sponge and quit in disgust.

Meanwhile some of the missionaries and workers connected with the Howard Mission had been exploring this moral wilderness, and among other noted apostles of vice, had fallen in with John Allen, the "Wickedest Man" of Oliver Dyer's article.

Allen was of respectable family, and a man of good intelligence, fair education, and considerable means. Two or three of his brothers were ministers of the Gospel. At this time he seemed to glory in the audacity and hardihood with which he sinned against light. His dance-house was a place of the vilest resort, and he ruled with an iron hand and a heart of stone the wretched women who inhabited it, and the hapless sailors and others whom they enticed into it. By some peculiar tact, aided by the mysterious influences of

Divine grace, the missionaries and the Christian gentlemen who accompanied them in frequent visits to this vile den, found their way to the good graces of its hardened master.

One day they proposed that he should permit them to hold a prayer-meeting that evening in his dance-hall. In a spirit of good-humored bravado he told them they might try it if they liked, and take the consequences, but refused to have anything to do with it himself. That evening, after the scraping of the fiddle and the shuffling of feet had ceased, one of them stepped quietly into the room, and kneeling in the middle of the sanded floor, said, "Let us pray;" and before the astonished company had taken in the meaning of the unwonted spectacle, he was pouring out, in a voice thrilling with emotion, his eyes streaming with tears, an earnest prayer to God for the souls of all present, from John Allen down to the wretched fiddler in his corner. The effect was magical. Instead of the expected scoffs and gibes which Allen had predicted, and which the brave mis-sionary had braced himself with the enthusiasm of martyr-dom to meet, there was utter silence for a few minutes, save the voice of prayer, and then a sob here and there, and finally tears and sobs all around that room, whose walls had heretofore echoed only the profane and obscene speech and the hollow laughter of undisguised licentiousness and riot.

These events marked the beginning of the "John Allen Excitement" as it was called, to which Jerry refers in his autobiography.

Allen himself so far yielded to moral and religious in-fluences as to become thoroughly ashamed of his wretched business, and to abandon it. He offered his house for reli-gious meetings, which for a while were continued there, took part in them himself, and expressed a desire for reformation and a better life. He was, after all, a man with a tender spot in his heart. He has come to me and told me of his struggles with the demons that had taken up their abode in his soul, and has laid his head on my shoulder and sobbed like a child, as he told me that he would give all he had in the world to bring back the pure influences of his childhood, and blot out the record of his sinful and debauched life. He was, however, a vain man, and courted the notoriety of being held up as a hard case reformed. He was saturated with vice and with the appetite for drink, and, although manifestly touched and moved, he did not seem to show those evidences of thorough reformation, and of the work of grace in his heart, which those interested in him hoped at one time to witness. He never went back to the miserable business in which he had been so long engaged, but opened a respectable grocery-store in Roosevelt Street, and died a few years afterward. It is not for human eye to discern, or human tongue or pen to say, that the influences of the remarkable religious outburst, in which he had unwittingly cut so conspicuous a figure, were lost upon him, or that on the banks of Jordan, or midway in its swelling stream, he did not meet and know the Saviour who had died for him, and hear repeated the gracious words that had opened the gates of Paradise to a dying thief on Calvary, eighteen hundred years before.

After meetings had been held in his dance-house for a while, it was thought best to transfer them to another place, and the lease of a neighboring notorious dance-house was bought out and the work transferred to it. This was No. 316 Water Street, where Jerry McAuley first publicly testified of salvation and where he afterward commenced his own work, and where the "McAuley Water Street Mission" now stands.

I have thought that the foregoing brief sketch of the beginning of active Christian work in Water Street would be of interest to many not familiar with its history, and would not be inappropriate here, on account of Jerry's reference to it, and its connection with his own restored life and his subsequent work for the Master in the same locality.

It seemed at that time to those who were actors in the scenes to which I have referred, almost as if a veritable miracle was being wrought in the opening to religious influences and work of this abandoned and vice-ridden part of the city; as if the Holy Spirit went before them and prepared the hearts of the godless throng who inhabited and frequented it, and held the mouths and hands of those who would before have cursed and stoned the messengers of the Gospel. I have myself spoken from the steps of John Allen's dance-house to a crowd filling Water Street almost from Roosevelt to Dover, and been listened to with quiet respect, where a few months before it would have been considered as much as a man's life was worth to attempt to hold a religious service in the open air. We held prayer-meetings in Kit Burns' rat-pit,—a rough amphitheatre in the rear of a bar-room,—with the dogs growling, and the rats squealing in their cages under the benches, while Kit's customers, thronging his bar-room, looked on in respectful silence, any tendency to the contrary being promptly suppressed by Kit himself.

11

CHAPTER XV.

RECOLLECTIONS CONTINUED.

' Christ first and last, Christ all day long,
My hope, my solace, and my song;
His love so full, so sweet, so strong.
Christ for me, Christ for me."

UNPROMISING as Jerry's appearance then was at first sight, there was something irresistibly winning about him, which at once awakened the interest of those who came in closer contact with him; and I became impressed, before I had known him long, with the sincerity of his purpose, and a sort of sturdy, manly independence and earnestness which characterized him. I saw a good deal of him, and we became fast friends.

One of the first evidences of the reality of the change which grace had wrought in him, and of the Divine light in his conscience, was a prompt confession that he and Maria were not man and wife, and a request for advice as to what they ought to do. "Be married," we said, "of course." 'Ah! there's the rub," said Jerry.

Further conversation developed the fact that there were reasons why their immediate marriage would not be expedient.

We then told him that they must live apart until Providence should open the way for their lawful union according to the ordinance of God. To this they readily assented.

Maria lived for a while in a Christian family in New Jersey, and afterward went to the home of her parents in another State and remained a while. When she came back, all obstacles having been by that time removed, they stood up together in the parlor of Howard Mission, and were solemnly joined in marriage, the writer and a few other friends being present.

I do not think I ever in my life assisted at a wedding which afforded me more genuine satisfaction. During Maria's absence, Jerry used sometimes to bring me her letters to read, and talk with me about their future hopes and plans; and in this way their sincere affection for each other sanctified by grace in their regenerated hearts, had been revealed to me. Their mutual devotion, and what they were to each other through all the trials and vicissitudes of their subsequent lives, and their final victory over their buried past in winning the confidence and respect of all who knew them, and until death parted them, does not need to be told.

The blunt and uncompromising honesty before God which the foregoing incident illustrates was one of the immovable planks in Jerry's religious platform.

"Be honest with God, and with yourself," he used to say to those professing repentance and desire for a better life, and yet seeming to be keeping something back; "you can't put off any humbugging lies on Him; you may cheat me, and maybe cheat yourself, but you can't cheat God. Turn yourself inside out, and make a clean breast of it."

There was little room in Jerry's heart for hatred of anything, after it became filled up with grace and with the spirit of the Master; but he did hate hypocrisy. This was about the only form of human weakness and depravity for which he did not have unlimited charity and compassion. He could not bear a hypocrite. It seemed as though he could not breathe with patience the air that was tainted with his presence; almost as though he had a kind of magnetic consciousness, that there was a hypocrite somewhere about, before he got within a block of the Mission. He always wanted to " fire them out" and keep them out.

This was about the only point on which Jerry and I ever split. I used to think sometimes that he was too hasty in his judgment, and too hard on those whom he thought were not honest. I used to tell him that he might mistake human inconsistency and the results of human weakness for hypocrisy, and that there was hope that even a hypocrite might be reached by Divine grace, if he kept coming to the meetings. We had some lively discussions about it, but I could never make much impression on his convictions in this respect. I had abundant occasion to admit that Jerry had an uncommonly keen scent for hypocrisy, and sham and fraud of every kind, and that his intuitions in detecting them were generally correct.

One night in Water Street a man who had come forward in the after-meeting was asked by Jerry, as his custom was, to pray for himself. He began praying in a conventional and stereotyped way, for all the poor sinners in the room, for the heathen, and for everything else but his own salvation. Jerry, feeling that the true ring was not there, kept still as long as he could, and then turning to the man, said, " Look here, my friend, you had better ask God to have mercy on your soul," in a tone that would have seemed harsh and unfeeling to any one who did not know as well as Jerry did the kind of man he was talking to.

Jerry and his wife both had a very vivid sense of the change which grace had wrought in their lives and lot.

I used to visit them in the humble lodgings, always scrupulously neat, in which they lived while Jerry was working at one thing and another that he could find to do, before the Mission was opened. I had taken tea with them one night,—they were living in Division Street then,—and after tea we sat talking, and they told me a great deal about their past lives. Their thoughts were all of the wonderful things that God had done for them, and their talk of the past seemed to bring home to them with renewed force that night the blessedness they were then enjoying. After relating some of the sad and bitter experiences which sin had brought them, Maria, looking around the homely but cheerful room, and then at Jerry, and then at me, drew a long breath, and with a happy smile and glistening eyes said, "Can it be possible this is *us* ?"

In those early days Jerry set an inestimable value upon every token of trust in him. He had been so long hunted and dogged and accustomed to the thought that he was an outcast and outlaw whom nobody would trust out of sight with the value of a cent, that it was a new and sweet experience to him *to be trusted.* What a moral invigorator a little timely confidence and reliance on his honor was to him, and may be to others in like circumstances, as illustrated in one or two incidents, was often referred to in his public testimonies. He used to say, after telling what a miserable wretch, and moral and physical wreck he was before Jesus picked him up, "Just look at me now [holding open his coat and making a comical gesture of looking himself over], I have everything a man could want. I have plenty to eat,

a good home and good clothes, and *I am respected and
trusted.* Think of Jerry McAuley, the biggest bum that
used to hang out around this ward, turned into a respectable citizen. Why, a few years ago, if a man with five dollars in his pocket met me coming down the street, he'd cross
over on the other side, and lucky for him too; but now I
go down town, walk into a big banking-house, take an arm-
chair, put up one leg over the other, *and talk with the boss*
as big as life; and they don't set any detectives to watch
me either, or send for a policeman to run me out. This is
what Jesus has done for me—made a man of me; and he
will do it for you too if you will let him."

While Jerry was out of work, before he got steady employment, he used to come to me once in a while to see if I
could put him on the track of something to do. One day I
said to him, "Jerry, I have got a job for you if you will take
it." His eyes brightened.

"I'll take anything that's honest," he said.

"Well, Jerry," I said, "I have got a little yacht down in
Gowanus Bay, that wants watching until I can sell it. Now
I want you to go and live on it, and take good care of it,
keep everything clean and in good order, and see that
nobody runs off with anything, and I will pay you $— a
month and your grub."

"Will you trust me to do that?" he said, with an expression on his face that, between what was to him the
comical side of anybody trusting him with valuable property, and the emotion which the idea of being trusted
awakened when he had fairly taken it in, was a study.
The unaccustomed luxury of feeling that he was trusted,
got the upper hand, and his eyes filled with tears.

The bargain was struck, and the next day Jerry took up

his quarters on the little vessel. The boat had a lot of sil-
ver-plated ware on board of no great value; but, as Jerry
told me afterwards, he thought it was " all solid silver, and
worth a mint of money;" and, knowing that Gowanus Bay
was infested with river thieves, he was greatly oppressed
with the responsibility, and used to lie awake nights with
his revolver cocked, and jump up and creep out on deck at
the slightest sound of the stealthy dipping of oars. He
told me afterwards that he was haunted with the fear that
something might be stolen from the boat, and that when it
was missed I would think he had betrayed his trust, and he
determined that if anybody got anything out of that boat,
it should be over his dead body. " After you had trusted
me, I couldn't stand it, you know, to have you think ill of
me, and I would have died first," he said. Jerry often
used to tell this story, portraying his anxieties and describing his night encounters with imaginary river-thieves, with
inimitable effect, and would say, " When I found I was
trusted like that by a man who knew all about my past life,
I began to respect myself and think, ' Jerry McAuley, there
is a chance for you after all, and you will be somebody yet
before you know it,' and it gave me a big boost."

It was some time before Jerry succeeded in getting steady
employment. He worked for a while on one of the ferries,
then as a 'longshoreman, then on a steamship dock, always
ready to turn his hand to anything by which he could earn
an honest living. The persecutions of godless fellow-workmen who mocked at his religion; the injustice of foremen
who encouraged them, and embraced every opportunity to
place him at a disadvantage; the requirement that he
should work on Sunday, and other like causes, drove him

out of these different employments one after another. These discouragements, however, never shook him from his purpose to live an honest life, and to live it according to the light with which the Holy Spirit had illumined his conscience.

After a while the writer found a vacancy for a porter in a sewing-machine establishment on Broadway, where he was well known, which he determined to secure for Jerry. The question which persons interested in procuring employment for ex-convicts have often found an embarrassing one naturally arose. Should I tell them frankly what he had been, and try to induce them to take him and trust him, with a full knowledge of his past criminal life, and his present purposes to serve God and be an honest man? Or should I suppress all this, and simply recommend him as a man in whom I had confidence, and trust to the chances of his past remaining unknown? I am aware that many good people have held opposite opinions as to the best course to be pursued in such cases. In Jerry's case it was decided *in what I believe to be the only right way, and the best and safest for the reformed man or woman in the end.* I talked with him about it; told him that, while it might be more difficult at first to find a place for him involving any trust or responsibility, if his story was frankly told, I was sure it would be better in the long-run to be square and open about it and trust God; that if he went into this place, for example, under false or concealed colors, some one might turn up at any time who had known him, and, pointing him out, whisper in the ear of his employers or his fellow-workmen that they were harboring and working side by side with a man who had worn the stripes and been behind the bars; when he would probably be turned out in disgrace, no matter how honest and faithful he had been, and be a marked man. Jerry fully agreed with me, and, with the unflinching honesty to which I have already referred, said, " I don't want any hiding or dodging. I won't be a fraud in any way, whatever else I am. I want to be just Jerry McAuley, and nothing else." I then went to the establishment mentioned, and told them frankly about Jerry's past life—who and what he was, and what I knew he was resolved hereafter to be. I told them what I had seen and known of his new life, and expressed my entire confidence in his sincerity and honesty. They looked grave at first, but became warmly interested in my account of Jerry. They hesitated, however, fearing that his past career would be discovered, and make trouble among the others. Finally I said, "Take him; trust him; make no attempt to conceal his history; let all your other men know that you know all about him, and have taken him for what he is, and I will be responsible for him; if he runs off with anything, send me the bill." They took him, and he remained in their employment until, in the enjoyment of the confidence and respect of the entire establishment, he left it to open the Mission in Water Street. When I told him, after he had been there a while, what I had said to them, and added laughingly, "If you should get away with a half-dozen truck-loads of sewing-machines some night it might break me," he said with an amused look, but with emotion, "You shall never be ashamed of me or sorry you said that. If the cellar where I work was a gold mine, or had diamonds lying all around loose, your promise should never cost you a cent."

While he was working there I used to call frequently to see him. He worked in the packing-room in the basement, which had an entrance down a flight of steps on the side

street.   When I wanted to see him I used to run in that
way.   One day I called, and did not see him in his usual
place.   I waited a while, and presently he came out from
behind a pile of packing-cases in one corner, with a radiant
face.   He said, " When I get lonesome and discouraged, and
feel the blues coming on, I go down on my knees behind
that great pile of boxes and pray, and then I am all right
again."

Jerry was passionately fond of singing, and had great faith
in its efficacy as a means of grace to the converts, and in its
power to attract those whom he sought to reach.   He
would say, when a verse of a hymn had not been sung to suit
him, " Try that again ; sing as if you meant it, and don't
go to sleep over it.   It will do you good.   Why, if people
should judge by the way you sung that verse they'd think
your religion was an awfully dull and up-hill business.   Now,
let's raise the roof;" and suiting the action to the word, he
would sing as if his whole soul and body went into the hymn.

Sometimes at the beginning of the meeting, when the
chapel was not filling up as fast as he would like to see it,
he would give out a hymn like " Pull for the shore," or
" Let the lower lights be burning," in which there was ample
scope for volume of sound, and say, " Open both the doors
there wide.   Now sing so they can hear you clear down to
Dover Street and up to James Slip."   And they did.

He was very impatient of long-winded harangues in a
testimony-meeting, and was inexorable in enforcing the
" one-minute rule" with which he had placarded the chapel,
even at the expense of giving offence to thin-skinned people
who were unused to his blunt ways and did not know

the wealth of tender solicitude for sinners that lay under-
neath his sharpest criticisms and his rudest speech. "These
long-winded fellows kill the meeting," he would say.
"Wind 'em up and set 'em a-going, and they don't know
when to stop. Now speak short. If you've come in here
with a long yarn all fixed up nice, with a beginning and a
middle and an ending, just cut off both ends and give us
the middle. I was a poor drunkard, a miserable loafer and
tramp, without a decent coat to my back, full of wickedness
and sin, and a terror around this terrible ward. Jesus
picked me up and saved me, and has kept me saved. Glory
to His name! There's my testimony, and it didn't take me
a minute to tell it either."

When his health began to fail and the trouble with his
lungs, the seeds of which had perhaps been sown in those
dreadful nights on the river, had begun to be serious, he
would sometimes, after an attack of pneumonia or a hemorrhage, almost literally crawl down-stairs to the meeting.
At such times he would say, with a tenderness and solem-
nity that filled our hearts with emotion and our eyes with
tears, "They say I've got only one lung and part of another.
I am weak and sore, and it hurts me sometimes to talk;
but I think of what the dear Jesus suffered for me, and
my heart is full. I am happy. Sometimes I think I can't
live very long; it seems as if my lungs were all gone; but
while I've got a piece of a lung left I want to use it to
speak for Jesus. I want to praise Him with my dying
breath."

He had a wonderful faith—a faith which was childlike in
its simple and confiding trust, yet firm as a rock. It was of

a very practical sort too. He believed in direct and specific answers to prayer, of which he had frequent and unmistakable experiences, and in the interposition of God in matters unseen and unknown by us until the need, and the divine hand supplying it, are revealed to us at the same time. Once the old building in Water Street needed some repairs, and when the plaster had been stripped off the ceiling, showing the ends of the beams all rotted away, Jerry said, "It seems as though God's hand held up that old second floor, for there was nothing else to hold it up;" and he believed it.

He was very persistent in whatever he undertook, in accordance with what he believed to be the will of the Lord. His obstinacy in the pursuit of anything to which he was persuaded that God had called him was beyond the power of human persuasion or reasoning to overcome.

When he felt that his work in Water Street was done, and that he was called to labor up-town, I did not think it was wise for him to leave Water Street, broken in health as he was, and assume the responsibilities and labors of a new enterprise; and I earnestly and honestly opposed it. But notwithstanding his love for me and his respect for my opinions my disapproval did not cause him to falter or waver for a moment, and the Cremorne Mission was the result.

I was afterwards glad to see and to acknowledge that Jerry's divinely-guided impulses were right, and that what I thought my cool-headed judgment was wrong.

His work and its influences were not limited to any particular class. His principal aim was the salvation of outcast men and women; for this he labored and thought and prayed; but his work had a reflex influence which spread out through all classes, and by means of it hundreds of refined and cultivated people were led to Christ, and a multitude of Christians were aroused and animated to higher and better lives, and to more earnest and believing work for Jesus.

He used to say, after exhorting the drunkards and those low down in sin to come to Jesus and be saved, and calling on the Christian people present to pray for them, "and don't let us forget the kid-glove sinners, who need it as bad as any of these poor fellows." "God is no respecter of persons," was one of his favorite sayings; and nothing delighted his heart more than to see a seal-skin sacque or a broadcloth coat, at the bench side by side with an old red shirt or a ragged and dishevelled dress, the wearers of both taking in the water of life from the same fountain.

Jerry's public speaking was often a curious mixture of pathos and wit, quotations from Scripture, and the vernacular slang of the class whom he addressed. The conventional notions of propriety of refined and fastidious Christians were sometimes startled and shocked by his quaint and blunt speech, his mimicry, his total disregard of the tones and manner which they had previously regarded as inseparable from proper and becoming religious speech, and his revelations of the sin and depravity of his past life; but when they came often enough to see how all this was signally blessed and honored of God to the salvation of men, their jealousy for the proprieties went down before their interest in the results.

I have frequently seen Christians restless and ill at ease,

and manifestly disturbed, as they listened for the first time
to one of his characteristic exhortations or testimonies, and
afterwards melted to tears, and swept into resistless sympathy with him, his work, his methods and all, as they
listened to one of his indescribably tender and touching
prayers over some sobbing penitent, and felt themselves
borne by it nearer to the cross of Christ and the gate of
heaven, than the studied rhetoric of the pulpit or the
dignified propriety of a church prayer-meeting had ever
brought them.

CHAPTER XVI.

MR. HATCH'S " RECOLLECTIONS."—*Concluded.*

" Grace all the work shall crown,
　　Through everlasting days;
　It lays in heaven the topmost stone,
　　And well deserves the praise."

IT would be difficult, if not altogether impossible, to so analyze Jerry's character or define the sources of his influence and success as to create out of them an available model upon which other regenerated roughs may be moulded into future Jerry McAuleys. His downright sincerity, his earnestness and singleness of purpose, his indomitable pluck and perseverance, and his devout piety are indeed alike worthy and susceptible of imitation by any man, whatever his past record may be, who yields himself up, as Jerry did, to the love and service of the Lord Jesus.

Those peculiarities and distinctive traits which went to make up his personality cannot be portrayed like the well-defined lines and curves of a mathematical figure, to be copied and reproduced at will. The coming transformed rough or criminal, who shall set out to become by imitation a second Jerry McAuley will probably prove a lamentable and ludicrous failure. He imitated no one; he was himself inimitable; he stands alone, a unique example of the Divine selection of material, which, in its rough state, it is safe to say, ninety-nine out of every hundred religious experts would have unhesitatingly rejected; and of what may be wrought by the grace of God and the love of Jesus out of and through the sort of stuff that Jerry was made of.

It is alike impracticable to formulate his methods, as a system or a plan of Christian work. He worked in his own way, in the only way in which it was possible for him to work, and in many respects as he alone could have worked successfully. He could not be pared down, or rounded off, or adjusted to any pattern set by another, or fitted to any conception that well-meaning friends may have entertained as to what he ought to be and do. He was Jerry McAuley by the grace of God, and as such let us be thankful for him.

His work, and that of the missions which bear his name and perpetuate his influence, and the undeniable success which even the severest critics of their direct and homely way of attacking sin and saving sinners have been compelled to recognize, have, however, given a new value to methods and instrumentalities which had previously been contemplated by many conservative and over-refined Christians with grave distrust, and in some cases even with undisguised contempt; and have imparted a new impulse to their use, in connection with missionary effort for the salvation of the lost and for the reclamation of those whom the more refined and stately ministrations of the pulpit have failed to reach.

The holding of nightly meetings throughout the year without interruption or break, where men and women burdened with sin, broken down and shattered by debauchery and vice, homeless and hopeless, hungry, ragged and defiled, drunk or sober, fresh from the prison or the gutter, are welcomed, are made to feel that somebody cares for them and that their wretched past has not made decency and respectability in this life and salvation in the

life to come impossible to them, and are taught that
Jesus died for *them* and that God loves them ; the direct,
unconventionial, blunt presentation of religious truth, in language which is familiar to the classes to whom it is addressed and the force of which they can appreciate; the
personal experiences and testimonies of those who have
been saved, carrying practical conviction and hope to the
hearts of others who are what the saved ones once were,
and persuading them that there is salvation for *them* also—
these are among the more prominent characteristics of
Jerry's work which have been so signally honored and
blessed of God to the salvation of many, and which have,
through it, become more conspicuous features in missionary
effort than ever before.

This is especially true of the practical preaching of the
Gospel of salvation through the personal testimonies of the
saved; and it has been found that, just as the personal
witness of a blind man whose eyes have been opened is
a more effective advertisement of the skill of the physician who opened them, to send other blind men to him,
than a whole volume of essays on the theory of blind-
ness and its cure, so the sincere and simple declaration, "I
was a drunkard, a gambler, a thief, homeless, ragged, despised and outcast, and Jesus picked me up and saved me,
and has made me respectable and happy, filled my soul
with peace, and opened to me the gates of Paradise," has
infinitely more power to attract the faith of others in like
wretchedness and despair to the Jesus who has done all
this, than a whole library of sermons on the nature of sin
and the theology of the plan of salvation.

Multitudes of Christians have felt their pride of culture
humbled, their refinements of taste in respect to religious
12

methods rebuked, and their sense of the power of Divine grace and of the superiority of infinite wisdom over human judgment in the selection and use of means, lifted up higher, as they have seen in Jerry's meetings how God has chosen the foolish things of this world to confound the wise, and the weak things to confound the mighty, and the base things and things which are despised, that no flesh should glory in his presence; and have learned in humiliation and shame for their past fastidiousness, that it ill becomes human frailty to despise or criticise or hold in light esteem that which God has honored and dignified.

In explanation of many of the testimonies which are heard in these Mission meetings, the following extracts from the report of an address delivered by the writer of these notes, at an anniversary of the McAuley Water Street Mission five or six years ago, may not be out of place.

The experience and observation of the intervening years, in intimate connection with work of this kind, has in no wise changed or modified the views then expressed.

———

" Although the testimonies given in these meetings are well understood by those who are familiar with them and with the personal histories of those who utter them, occasional visitors from an entirely different condition in life, and accustomed to quite another phase of religious experience, may sometimes misapprehend them and question the genuineness of the spiritual experiences of which they are the expression.

" It is difficult for Christians whose position and circumstances in life when converted were those of respectability and comfort to realize all that religion—salvation through the Lord Jesus Christ—means to many of these people whose testimonies are to be heard there. While it means to them the same cleansing from sin, the same inward peace, the same hope of heaven, that it means to others; it means to many of them, in addition to all this, much more besides. To many of them it means, not only reconciliation to God, but also reconciliation to human laws and to human society. To some of them it means no more fear of the policeman's grip or the detective's stealthy tread; no more dread of the prison and the gallows; no more weeks in the Tombs; no more months on Blackwell's Island; no more dreary years at Sing Sing or Auburn. To them it means an honest life; the confidence and trust of their fellow-men; liberty to walk upright in broad day, unhunted, and without a price upon their heads; and the sweetness of eating in fearless security the bread of honest toil!

"To many others it means no more dreadful carousals in beastly drunkenness; no more bruised and aching heads; no more smashed crockery and mutilated furniture; a wife broken-hearted no more; and their children fleeing from them no more in terror! It means no more journeys to the pawn-shop; no more homeless wanderings in the streets by day; no more sleepless nights in station-houses, or in dirty dens, or on the docks, or in the gutters!

"To these men and women salvation means decent clothing instead of rags, cleanliness instead of dirt and vermin. It means parents reconciled, home restored, wife and children happy and smiling. It means food and raiment and employment and friends and self-respect, and everything else that makes human life comfortable and happy. We need not wonder, therefore, that, in attempting to tell what Jesus has done for them, they speak of these things. Good Christian people, coming as visitors to these meetings, and

hearing these testimonies but once, or only at long inter-
vals, are sometimes disturbed with the fear that these men
and women are not soundly converted. Hearing them, in
the fulness of their gratitude, and in the warmth of their
love, tell of the homes, the friends, the food, the clothing,
the good wages, and the comforts of life which the service
of God has brought to them, the stranger may sometimes
say, 'Why, these people seem to value salvation only for the
material comforts and rewards which it brings to them!'

"We who know them, and hear them often, know better
than this. When they speak here, they are limited in their
testimonies to one minute, in order that as many as possible may have an opportunity to speak at each meeting. A
man cannot tell all that he feels and knows of the love of
God and of the blessings of salvation in one minute. One
has to hear them ten, twenty, fifty times, before all that
they have to tell of the goodness of God and the happiness
of serving their new-found Master and Redeemer comes
out. I have heard some of them testify a hundred times;
and each time have found that not half the story of their
redemption had yet been told. And we who have heard
their testimonies most frequently, and know their hearts
and their lives best, have found that those who have the
most grateful sense of these present blessings and material
benefits, which the love and service of Jesus have brought
into their lives, and who speak first and often of these
things, have also the strongest faith in God, the sweetest
experiences of inward peace and spiritual communion with
him, and the brightest and most stedfast hope of eternal
life.

"These testimonies show that if there is one truth of the
Gospel more clearly illustrated in the experiences of the

people converted in this mission than another, it is that 'godliness is profitable unto all things, having promise of the life that now is, and of that which is to come.' To the poor, wretched, homeless wrecks of body and soul, that drift into the meetings, the truth is preached in every testimony: 'It pays in this life to serve Jesus.'

"It is of but little use to preach this truth to the well-to-do sinner, surrounded by wealth, friends, and all the comforts of life. He thinks that he already has the 'promise of the life that now is.' Salvation means to him self-sacrifice, a surrender of some of the riches, pleasures, and self-indulgences in which he revels. To move him to repentance and godliness, you must appeal to his conscience, and his duty to his Maker, and must turn the current of his thoughts to 'that life which is to come.' But to many of the outcasts who wander into these meetings there is little need to preach of a heaven and a hell hereafter ; for when they come in sorrow and penitence to the Lord Jesus, and surrender themselves to Him, they are fleeing from a present hell on earth ; and when they are converted a heaven begins to them right here and now.

"Their most frequent thoughts and expressions, therefore, are not so much about the penalties of sin and the rewards of righteousness in the life to come, as about this truth— which has been revealed to them—that 'godliness is profitable unto all things, having promise of *the life that now is.*' To them the dividing line in human existence is not so much the grave separating between time and eternity, as it is the hour in which they were lifted up out of a visible hell on earth, into what is to them a present heaven, and began to enjoy the 'promise of the life that now is.'

"Afterward, when they have come to realize the terrible

abyss of eternal woe from which the blood of Jesus has redeemed them, and their hearts begin to take in some conception of the things which God hath prepared for them
that love Him, then their faith lifts itself up and takes hold
on eternal realities, and they learn the higher strains of the
song of redemption. But they never cease to remember
and to testify that it is Jesus who, in saving them from sin
now, has saved them from the wretchedness and shame
which sin had brought into their lives."

The preparation of the foregoing sketch has been a labor
of love. Its purpose, however, has not been merely to en-
circle the head of Jerry McAuley with a glory, after the
manner of the old masters in adorning their canvas with
saintly figures; nor to throw a halo of romantic interest
around his life and work; but rather to seek to bring into
stronger light, if possible, some of the practical lessons
which they suggest.

If it shall reawaken in the heart of any lost and despairing sinner, hopes long overlaid with sin and buried out of
sight and consciousness under the wreckage of a reckless
and debauched life; or if it shall give an encouraging impulse to any, who, having been born into the kingdom of
God out of the rough places in life without education or
previous Christian training and burdened with a sense of
their lack of those requirements which go to make up a conventional outfit for usefulness, are sorrowfully asking " What
can I do for Jesus?"; or if it shall serve to stimulate any of the
Christian men or women into whose hands the providence
of God may bring it, to more believing and earnest work for
the salvation of those whom, perhaps, they have hitherto
considered beyond hope—its highest aim will have been
fulfilled. A. S. H.

CHAPTER XVII.

EVERY EVENING IN WATER STREET.

Hark ! how the blood-bought hosts above
Conspire to chant the Saviour's love,
  In sweet harmonious strains !

We'll join the song ! for we can tell
How sovereign grace dissolved the spell,
  That kept us bound in chains ;
And from that dear and happy day,
How oft we've been constrained to say
  That grace triumphant reigns !

In the year 1880 a pamphlet entitled " Down in Water
Street Every Evening" was prepared by Mr. William R.
Bliss of this city. The little work gives a graphic portrait
of the Water Street meetings as conducted by Jerry that is
worthy of being recorded in more permanent form. That
part of its contents has, therefore, with slight condensation,
been copied, and is presented in the two following chapters.
It was the custom then, as it is now, after a brief service of
song, to offer prayer for divine blessing, and then to read
from God's Word. This done, Jerry would introduce the
testimonies by giving his own. These are his words as given
in the pamphlet mentioned :

" The meeting is now open for testimonies. Every one
who wants to speak for the Saviour can have one minute to
speak in. There are a good many here that have got reason
to testify what the Lord has done for them. Now don't be

afraid to do it! Stand right up, young converts! Jesus
said, 'Whosoever shall confess me before men, him will I
confess before my Father in heaven.' Stand up and confess him, and it will give you a good boost towards heaven
every time you do it. Speak short, or you'll rob somebody
else of a chance; long-winded speeches will kill a meeting
quicker than lightning! If any of you feel like making a
long speech, just cut off both ends and give us only the
middle of it!

"I'll tell you my experience, and I won't be long about
it. This blessed Jesus saves me. He saves me to-night
from being a drunkard, and a gambler, and a thief, and a
fraud, and everything else that you can put in. He saved
me eleven years ago; and he saves me more to-night than
he did then, because I've grown in grace. Bless his holy
name forever! When I tell you that Jesus saves me, I
mean just what I say! There's no sham about it! I don't
tell you I was a drunkard, and a thief, and a fraud, to glory
in it. But I want you rough men to understand what Jesus
has done for me. Yes, when I was such a miserable sinner
that I hadn't a friend, this blessed Jesus picked me up out
of the mud, and saved me from desiring to do those things
which I had been doing. And he saves me now. Who
wouldn't love the name of Jesus? The meeting is open."

Two or three immediately stand up to speak.

This man, thirty-two years old, was born and brought up
in Water Street; became a fearless and desperate burglar;
and came into the chapel for the first time about two years
ago, direct from the New Jersey State Prison. He says:

"If there's any unfortunate wretch here to-night, down
deep in crime as I was, I want him to know what Jesus has
done for me. My heart sometimes fills right up when I

THE HELPING HAND.
The Old Building, 316 Water Street.

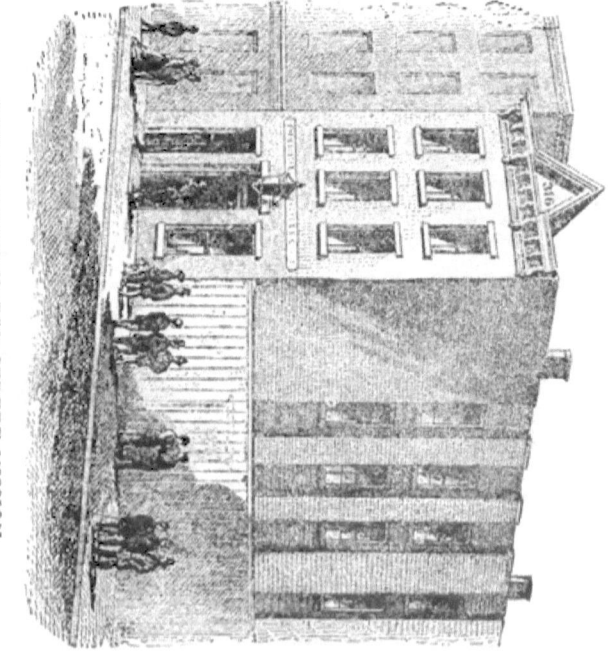

THE McAULEY WATER STREET MISSION.
The New Building, 316 Water Street.

think about it. I've been through all kinds of sin. I never was intemperate. But I've been a desperate man, and I've committed the worst crimes. I've been twice in State prison. Many were the sad, sad years I've spent alone behind the prison bars! I thank God that I ever came into this Mission! I came here looking for work. I didn't want religion: I wanted an honest job. I listened to the testimonies, and I saw that the men were in earnest; and when Jerry gave the invitation to come forward for prayers, I went. I knelt down and prayed. I couldn't grasp the meaning of it. But God in mercy heard me, and how he has blessed me since! When I first came in here, I had just been serving a term of seven years and seven months out of ten years. The man that went in with me got twenty years, and it was only by the mercy of God that I didn't get it!

"But Jesus has forgiven my sins, and has made me a happy, peaceful, and contented man, which I never was before. Once I was afraid to go through the streets by daylight lest the first policeman I met should tap me on the shoulder and say, 'I want you!' But now I can look any man square in the face and feel that I am honest, and am trying to do what is right in the sight of God. My friends, if I didn't know there's a reality in this religion I'd chuck it up! I wouldn't stand here talking in this way; and my only object in telling this is to induce some man who has been as bad as I was to come to Jesus and be saved from his sins."

A 'longshoreman says:

"Jesus saves me to-night from being a drunkard, a gambler, a thief, and every sinful habit. He has taken the desire for sin away from my heart, because I ask him to do it every day. A little more than six years ago I and my wife were good-for-nothing drunkards. What we had on our backs when we first came into this Mission, put together, wouldn't have fetched fifty cents in a junk-shop. Blessed be God, it isn't so now! If you knew what my home was six years ago, and see it to-night, you'd say I've got out of hell into heaven! My old friends alongshore told me they'd give me to hold on until I'd got a dollar to spend. But, blessed be God, I haven't gone back yet! What is there to go back to? Jesus keeps me, and he has sweetly kept me and my wife for six years and a little more. Every promise in the Bible has been fulfilled in my case. Although I used always to steal sugar regularly from vessels I was discharging, I haven't stolen the value of one pin from any man for more than six years, and haven't desired to! Blessed be God for this salvation! Christian friends, pray for me."

This man's testimony has suggested the singing of

> " What a friend we have in Jesus,
>   All our sins and griefs to bear," etc.

His wife follows him, saying:

" Six years ago there was never a more degraded sinner than I was, to my shame be it said. My home was a drunkard's hovel, and the principal thing there was the rum-bottle. I kept coming to this Mission, but there was so much Romanism rooted and grounded into me that it took a long time for me to be willing to let Jesus in. But I can now say, to the glory of God, that my sins are all forgiven, and the past is under the Blood. In place of the rum-bottle we have the Bible in our home, and it isn't kept for ornament; and if God calls us at any time, we are all packed up and ready to go."

The young man now speaking is a steam-engineer, accustomed to earn fifty dollars a month. For ten years he spent all his earnings in the rum-shops of Water Street and its neighborhood :

"I do thank God that I ever came into this Mission ! It has made a man of me ! I knew about it for years before I came in ; but I preferred to spend my evenings in those places on the corners over there. I never had a white shirt, nor an overcoat, or any comfort or happiness, before I came here, although I had money enough. I hadn't written my mother for nine years, but when I began to come here I wrote to her about it. I earn less wages now than I did when I was serving the devil ; but I have got more, because I don't use it to support the rum-sellers, and I don't spend any of it in sin. Jesus saves me and keeps me every day ; and oughtn't I to be thankful for it ?"

This man is a graduate of Dartmouth College, where, he says, he acquired his intemperate habits because he was allowed too much money by his parents. He has practised law in Massachusetts. Intemperance brought him to New York, and he had been entirely abandoned by all, family and friends, except his wife, when by chance he strolled into the Mission from a low grog-shop in Chatham Square, where he was existing:

"It is not long that I have been coming to these meetings. When I think of what I am now and what I was last summer, I am astonished. I had nothing then. I have everything that I need now. When my last cent was gone I told my companion if he would go and sell my old linen coat we'd take a drink with the money. When he brought me the money I thought we had better get something to eat, as we had not had anything for two days. So we went and got two bowls of soup. That night I strayed into this Mission, and I have not drunk any liquor since ! The other day I met my old companion, and he wanted to treat me. ' What will you take?' said he. Said I, ' I'll take a box of paper collars, as I need some; but no more rum for me!' The Lord Jesus has saved me, and I desire to serve him."

Another who was converted here, but is now living in a Western town, has come in to express his gratitude:

" I can look back more than six years to the blessed Sabbath when God first sent me into this Mission, and began his work in my heart. I began my drinking career on Broadway, then drifted into the Bowery, and had got down into Water Street when the Mission arms caught me. I was thinking about it to-day, and I shuddered as I looked and saw how few steps more it was to the river! I realize how very narrow was my escape from destruction! God has been good to me in many ways, and, best of all, he has kept me in the straight path."

A pale-faced man, recently from prison, says:

" I was a criminal from boyhood. My first sentence to prison was when I was nine years old. I have served four terms in prison. When I happened to come into this meeting one night—and I was received with open arms—I was tired of sin, tired of eating bread and water behind the bars. The testimony I heard, together with the words of Mr. McAuley, had a reaction on my mind. I knelt down and prayed, and my sorrows were healed. I now have a vocation, and I love my Saviour."

A young man who works in a printing-office follows:

" I am only twenty-two years old. I was a drunkard four years: in Albany, and Boston, and this city. Being a compositor by trade, I got work wherever I went. But my wages all went for drink, and at last I became an inmate of a low den in Chatham Square. For months I scarcely left it; when I got stupidly drunk I went into the back room and slept on the floor, with forty or fifty others like myself. My bed was a couple of newspapers, and a cheese-box for a pillow. I was going such a way that I'd have turned up my toes in a month or two longer, if I hadn't come in here. One Sunday evening I thought I would go down here and listen to the singing. When the invitation was given to come forward for prayers, I went. And I went a good many times afterwards. I was a Roman Catholic, and it seemed hard work for me to get changed. But at last Jesus extended his hand, and led me out of darkness into light. He keeps me daily by simply trusting him."

This large man, with a beaming face, is the captain of a three-masted schooner :

"It's very hard work to sit still here! There's no one in this room who has more reason to bless God than I have ; and I should do injustice to the dear Lord if I should not give my testimony. I feel that I owe all that I am to-night, in answer to my mother's prayers. At fourteen years of age I went to sea, as my father had done ; and I never shall forget that my mother kneeled down with me before I went away, and she prayed, 'O Lord, keep my son from temptation; he goes out to take his father's place.' The dear Lord followed me to sea. He has saved me from sin, and given me a clean heart; and he gives me the evidence, every day I live, that I am born of God; that I am an heir of heaven! I am so glad to recommend this same Jesus to every sinner. Yes; blessed be his name! He can save if we will only let him."

The man now rising to speak is a steamship officer :

"I thank God for ever having let me come to this Mission. When I was a youth I went to sea, and soon learned to sin ; I used to get drunk, and had a sore head and a sore heart all the time. I didn't have a friend in the world. I never lived right until God led me into this place. When I gave Jesus my heart he saved me from my sins, and they are no more to me. He has taken everything wicked out of my desires. Jesus is my Saviour, and I don't do the things I used to do, because he saves me. I know it is good to be a servant of Jesus. I know it is hard to be a servant of the devil. Since I've been serving God I've never had to look for a ship. I ought to be thankful, indeed ; and I hope you will pray for me. I'm far from what I ought to be."

> "I need thee every hour,
> Most gracious Lord," etc.,

is now sung.

This man is a truckman for the Bridgeport steamers:

" My testimony to-night is that Jesus saves me. I had a good home once, and a good mother who prayed for me. But I slammed the door in her face ; and for nine years I gave all my earnings to the gin-mills, and had to go a-begging and to prison. I heard about this Mission one night in a thieves' den in the Bowery. I wasn't sober when I first came in here. The clothes I had on—some belonged to my father and some to my brother. I didn't suppose I was worth saving. I didn't know that anybody cared for me. I heard the testimonies of men who had been drunkards and thieves, like as I was. I thought I'd try to get this salvation ; and I did. I went out of here that night a sober man. Some ladies at the door shook hands with me and asked me to come again. It touched my heart. I hadn't received any such kindness since I left my mother. For nearly three years now I've had the evidence in my heart that I am saved. I have been living careless lately; but by the help of God I'll live so no more."

This young man came here from Sing Sing prison. There are sometimes fifteen or twenty men in a meeting who, like him, have been " behind the bars":

" I am one of those Christ came to save. I want to tell how he has saved me from my sins. When I first heard the testimony of these men here, telling how they were drunkards and thieves, and all that, I wasn't sober myself. I sat off there by the door. But I heard what the men said, and I said to myself, 'That's my life to a cent!' I was arrested in the street right opposite here, and I got five years in Sing Sing. I got the shower-baths, and the ball and chain, there. I was in a lot of fellows that tried to escape from prison on a raft. We got caught. One of· 'em was shot. If I'd been shot I know I'd been in hell to-night. When he was a-dying he asked me to pray for him. I didn't know how to pray! Never prayed in my life till I came into this Mission; and when I was invited I bounced right up for prayers. I didn't wait. Jesus heard my prayer, and I feel he has saved me. I know it. I like to come to the front and tell it now, because there are some fellows coming here that's just the kind I was, and I know Jesus can save 'em from their sins if they want to be saved. I never was happy till Jesus saved me."

This is an Erie Canal boatman now speaking:

"I bless God, to-night, that I have got an experimental religion. The religion of Jesus is a religion that I can talk about! I haven't had it but a short time, but it fills me with joy and peace every day; and God being my helper, I will tell of His saving grace as long as I live."

Then a man rises and says in a quiet tone:

"My dear friends: I want to say that when I first came in here, about four years ago, I was a poor lost drunkard, without a coat to my back or shoes to my feet. I know I was a nuisance everywhere. I wasn't worth ten cents; and I was ready to fight any man that put his fist in my face. But, my dear friends, it isn't so now. God has given me and my wife clean hearts and clean ways, and everything that we need, and has given me a humble and quiet spirit; and he has made us civil. If a man now strikes me on one cheek I think I am willing to turn to him the other also, if thereby I can serve God. I swing my sledge every day at my work with heavenly thoughts, and sometimes I forget my mate on the other side of the anvil, and keep striking as if it was one more blow for Jesus. My Christian friends, pray for me that I may ever be humble and faithful."

A young man, who has spent many years in prison, says, in an unpretending manner:

"I am thankful that God gives me a disposition to tell what he has done for me. I thank him for keeping me to-day in a time of temptation. I thank him for bringing me in here to-night, and not letting me roam around the streets as I used to do, committing all kinds of crimes. I want you all to pray for me."

Another now rises and says:

"I am glad to testify that Jesus saves me from my sins. How thankful I ought to be! He saves me from gambling and the use of tobacco and rum, and from everything that is wicked and sinful. He makes me a clean Christian."

He is followed by a captain of a tug-boat, saying:

"When I came in here a few months ago, the testimonies pricked me to the heart, and I didn't have any rest until I went to Jesus. Now I can say, 'For me to live is Christ, to die is gain.' I seek his blessing and guidance every morning before I start my boat, and every night after I have tied her up. I am trusting in him all the time."

This speaker is an officer of a sailing-ship:

"Friends," he says, "I've been following the sea all my life. When I wore ship and began to sail under the Lord's directions my shipmates said, 'You just wait and see how soon you'll get fetched up with a round turn.' But, thanks be to God, I haven't been fetched up yet! Jesus keeps me. He guides me with his counsel. He is the confidence of the ends of the earth, and of them that are afar off upon the sea."

We sing

        "He leadeth me! O blessed thought!" etc.,

when a sailor rises and says:

"I've been a desperate man, but now I'm a sinner saved by grace. I came along here and I heard the testimonies in the meeting. I reckoned the men were honest, and I made up my mind to wear ship and sail in the Lord's service. Ho! shipmates, there is no service like that! Bless the Lord! I've squared my yards by the lifts and braces, and I'm bound to glory now!"

Another sailor says:

"The first night I went away from this place I went aboard my ship and kneeled down in my cabin, and prayed the Lord to save me from my sins. And when he saved me I felt as my ship might feel when all the barnacles have been scraped off from her: I felt as if I had been scraped off clean inside and outside."

Then an old woman, with an Irish accent, says:

"This blessed Jesus saves old women too! I was a
13

drunken old thing, and told lies, and lived in a dirty hole, and had nothing. Thanksgiving night my four years was up since I first came in here. I was drunk then, but I haven't been drunk since, and never will be, God helping me! The Almighty God is good to me in everything. He sent me a turkey Thanksgiving Day, with money tied to the end of it, and I had turkey for seven days. When I came to Jesus I hadn't two cents in my pocket. Now, blessed be God! I've got a clean home, and a carpet and pictures, and I wouldn't be ashamed to ask any lady to come in there; and I've got a clean heart inside too! But I have to watch and pray. Mr. McAuley told me never to go to my bed without praying to the dear Jesus that saves us all, and to pray every morning ; and I do. If there's anybody here that don't love Jesus, they can't do better than kneel down and pray to him. Jesus can save you, and he can take care of you, too."

A German woman, who lives on a gravel-scow, says:

" Jesus saves me, too. I was a very bad woman a good many years. I cursed, I sold rum, and I quarrelled with everybody. I had a wicked temper. When the fire wouldn't burn in my stove, I kicked it, and I tore up my Bible, which I brought from Germany, to kindle the fire! I was good for nothing when I came in here. But, my dear friends, Jesus has taken me up and forgiven my sins and made me happy. I wouldn't go back on Jesus ; not for fifty dollars a week! Jesus gives me more, because He gives me all I need. There's nothing good for me to have that the Lord doesn't give it to me. He gives me my daily bread, and what do we need more? We didn't carry nothing into the world and we can't carry nothing out. One morning we had no bread, and my husband had no work. I went out

to look for work.   I ought to have taken a pail with me,
but I took a basket, and I stood on the corner and I prayed,
'Jesus, help me!'   Then I went to Sixth Avenue, and a
man came up and said, 'My good woman, do you want
some work?'   I said, 'Yes, sir.'   He said, 'What have you
got a basket for?'   I said, 'I don't know; but my husband
has no work and nothing to eat.'   He said, 'Can you scrub
my store?'   I said, 'Yes, sir.'   When I got through he filled
up my basket with bread and potatoes, and he put on top
a leg of mutton, and told me to come to-morrow!   Jesus
takes care of us.   He gives me a good home, and he makes
me and my husband happy all the time."

CHAPTER XVIII.

WATER STREET MEETING—*Concluded.*

> "He loveth me; O joy divine!
> Celestial light doth round me shine,
> And though unworthy I may be,
> I know that Jesus loveth me."

THE man now speaking is a truckman:

"I was once as bad a man as there was in this ward. But I had a praying mother, and God heard her prayers at last, when I got so low that I couldn't help myself. I had plenty of money once, but I spent it all for rum. When I first came into this Mission I was without a dollar, without a friend, and without a home. I had nothing but hard knocks; but I've got a good home now, and everything I need. I have made some sad falls since I began to serve the Lord, but I trust I have been forgiven."

A young man says:

"I thank the Lord Jesus that he saves me to-night from being in a rum-shop, or down in a ditch with somebody beating my eyes out. He gives me a desire to be with God's people."

Immediately another says, with tears in his eyes:

"When I first came in here I wasn't fit to be seen. I was a perfect wreck. Nobody would have anything to do with me—not even my family. I was such an outcast. But Jesus has saved me, and kept me now nearly two years.

What a Saviour that is who takes you up after everybody else has thrown you down! I'm so thankful to him! I wonder at myself when I think of the change the blessed Jesus has made in me and my home. He has given me a home that's a perfect heaven on earth!"

Then another young man says:

"I never shall forget the night of October 18, 1879, when the Lord Jesus gave me a new heart in this room. He has suppressed my appetite for intoxicating drinks. He helps me to resist temptation, and he makes my life all sunshine."

A man, who speaks with difficulty, rises and says:

"I was brought up with the roughest men; there was a gang of twelve of us; three of 'em have been hung. I lived right round here; knew all about sin; never knew anything about God; didn't care. Got up and went to bed every day just the same. Sometimes was cruising round all night. I had a little boy that died. I loved my boy; never loved anything else so much. I felt bad when he died; sat looking at him in the coffin, and thought about death. Then somebody came along and gave me a little book what told about this Mission. I read two pages of testimonies; I began to think about God. I came here to get that same religion. I've been coming ever since. I was in the house that stood here in '49—a dance-house. I was a boy thirteen years old then. Thank God, I have a Saviour now for twenty-one months. I'm sending my children to school to learn what their father didn't know. I'm fetching up my children in the fear of the Lord."

A man rises and announces himself as a stranger:

"I never was in here before, but going by the door I heard the singing, and thought I'd come in. I believe the Holy Spirit is working in me, and gives me courage to stand up. I had a good, praying mother. I ran away from her nineteen years ago, when I was seventeen years old, and I haven't seen her since. I've been a drinker, and a wanderer all about the world. These testimonies touch my heart. I feel a desire to live a better life. I want to ask you to pray for me that I may be saved."

Prayers are offered on this request; and then we sing—

> "Come, ye sinners, poor and needy,
>   Weak and wounded, sick and sore;
> Jesus ready stands to save you,
>   Full of pity, love, and power;
> He is able, He is willing; doubt no **more.**"

This young man has been well educated:

"I never knew what it was to be poor, until I became a drunkard. I have been a journalist; for several years I was proof-reader in the Government Printing Office at Washington. I lost my position through the use of alcoholic drinks, and when I first came into this room—well, a scarecrow, with any respect for his calling, would have blushed at me; would have left his place in the corn-field and walked out when he saw me coming! I had been on a spree for seven weeks; was in rags, houseless, homeless, and friendless. I was impressed with the sincerity and earnestness of the testimonies I heard here. I found sympathizing friends here. To-night I rejoice in a Saviour, and have in my heart the evidence of sins forgiven. I am now eight weeks old in the Christian life, and I pray that I may be faithful to the end."

This speaker is a companion of the last. They came to the Mission together, from a rum-shop in Chatham Square, where they had spent most of their time; ten of their com-

panions in that place have followed them here, one after the
other, and all are living the new life.

" It is now nearly eight weeks since I gave my heart to
God ; and when I remember all his loving-kindness to me,
my heart is full.   I was a miserable drunkard, cast off by
my family, and had no object in life except to get money to
spend for liquor.   I came here from curiosity one evening,
and, being vividly impressed by the testimonies, I went forward when the invitation was given, and on my knees asked
God to forgive me for the past.   He mercifully heard my
prayer.   He has taken the desire of strong drink away from
me, and given me assurance that I am one of his children.
Jesus is very precious to me every day.   I ask to be remembered in your prayers."

This speaker is another convert from the same place :

" I shall never forget the night when I first entered that
door—all broken up, good for nothing, without hope and
without friends.   I had been serving the devil for forty-two
years.   I graduated number one in his school.   What did
he do for me?   He left me without five cents in my pocket !
I see some of my old companions standing near the door
there now.   You needn't drop your heads down ; you
needn't feel ashamed to be here !   It was here I first found
hope and encouragement.

" If you will give me an extra minute, I would like to tell
a short story connected with my new life :

" About twelve months ago a motherless girl, only fourteen years of age, whose father was a drunken outcast on
the streets of New York, became a Christian.   Soon after,
she called on a Christian lady, and said, ' I have read in the
Bible that where two or three are met together in Christ's
name, there he is also.   I want to ask the privilege to have

a prayer-meeting in your house every morning before I go
to school, to pray for my father ; and as God may not know
whose father we are praying for, let us repeat his name in
every prayer.' For months they prayed, but God did not
answer. At last, on the night of the 28th of September,
1879, that father wandered into this Mission, and knelt weeping in penitence, asking God for Christ's sake to pardon his
sins. That child was my daughter, and to-night I thank
God that I have found the way of salvation."

This man is a marble-polisher :

" It will take a long time to tell what Jesus has done for
me. It's nigh three-and-twenty months since I first came
into this Mission. I wasn't sober then. I had just stolen
the last penny that my wife had in the house. When I
came in that door, I thought I was coming into a sing-song
place. My oldest girl, eleven years old, never slept on a
bed until after I came here. The children laid down on a
bundle of rags in the corner and got up ready-dressed in the
morning, because they slept in their clothes. You ought to
see my wife and children now, if you want to know what a
change the religion of Jesus has made in my home. To-
night Jesus saves me from being a drunkard, a gambler, and
a thief. I thank God that I am now what he intended me
to be—an honest laboring man. I can go through the
streets to-night a free man in Christ Jesus."

A young man who speaks very earnestly, says:

" When I first came in here I was almost dragged up to the
front; but I'm glad to come to the front now. I'm so glad
this religion is free to all. I'm so glad it's as good for the
drunkard as for the moral man. When God called Noah to
make the ark, he done it just as much for the mosquito as
for the elephant. When my mother died I was drunk. I

went to look at her dead body. I kissed her cold lips, but I couldn't shed a tear. But when Jesus showed me my heart I could cry. I was in prison Thanksgiving Day a year ago. But now Jesus saves me, and feeds and takes good care of me. Pray for me."

A young man says, with emotion:

"I shall never forget Thanksgiving night, 1879, when I first came in here. I was a drunkard. If I ever had a good thought I took a drink to wash it out. I found friends and the Saviour here. Now I'm drinking from heaven, and don't thirst any more."

Another rises and says:

"I can testify to-night for Jesus, that his yoke is easy and his burden is light."

Another man says:

"When I came into this Mission, two years and eight months ago, I was a poor lost drunkard. I hadn't hardly any shoes on my feet. Now I'm not in want of shoes or anything else. I can't thank the dear Jesus enough for what he has done for me. He gives me peace and joy in my heart all the time."

This man is employed in Jersey City:

"My dear friends, I once led a wild and reckless life. I came into this Mission three years ago and gave my heart to my Saviour. I erected a family altar in our home. It is a regular little paradise now. We always used to have a fight and tumble down before we went to bed. Now we always have prayers."

His wife rises and says:

"I thank God for the patience he had with me in my wicked life, and for saving me now. I praise his holy name to-night, and I pray that he will always keep me humble."

A young man says:

"I thank God when I think what I am and what I was eleven months ago. After trying repeatedly to save myself, I gave my heart to God, and he has made a new man of me. When I started I found the road kind of hard on account of being brought up a Catholic. But I learned to take everything to Jesus, and found him always ready to hear my prayer. I once had a strong appetite for drink, and I got so I couldn't earn enough to satisfy it, and I became dishonest and had to serve a couple of terms in prison. But I thank God I am a'free man now in Christ Jesus."

This man, about fifty-four years old, has spent more than half his life in eleven different English and American prisons. He says:

"This blessed Jesus saves me from being a thief. My parents were thieves. When I was eight years old I was in the same prison with my mother and aunt. I was transported to Van Diemen's Land for seven years, and I've got on my back the marks of the floggings I received there, nigh forty years ago, for trying to run away. I kept on stealing, and was sent to Australia for ten years; and when I got out I was stealing again, and they sent me to Gibraltar for five years. I was three years in a solitary cell, and never came out! God gave me health and strength, and in all the times I was coming out of prison I tried not to steal any more, but I had stealing on the brain. When I came into this Mission, on the 18th day of March, 1878, I was just down from Sing Sing, where I had been doing four years. But God has taken the desire for stealing out of my heart and put a better desire there; and I haven't had a thought to steal since. I am trying to serve God now. I ask an interest in all your prayers."

This man is a porter in a warehouse:

"There is, therefore, no condemnation to them who are in Christ Jesus, who walk not after the flesh, but after the Spirit; and I am glad to-night to testify that there is no condemnation for me! Jesus Christ is a perfect Saviour. He saves me completely. I feel the truth of that in my heart every day, and we can all have the witness of the Spirit in our hearts at any time if we only let Jesus give it to us. I thank God that I am not knocking around this ward to-night, as I was three years ago, beating some fellow-man and spending my evenings in lager-beer saloons, drinking and cursing, and taking God's name in vain. Oh, blessed be God for this salvation which is free to all!"

This man, a Swede, has been connected with the Mission's work for several years. He says:

"My youth was spent in smuggling. At the age of fourteen I lost a beloved brother in that nefarious business, which changed my way of life and sent me to sea from London. I was convicted of sin while on board the ship Black Adder, in Shanghai River, after I had challenged a man to fight. God's Holy Spirit touched me, and I resolved to lead a better life. After three months the Lord sweetly forgave me while I was working ballast in the ship's hold at Hong Kong, and to-night he saves me."

The testimonies are ended by the singing of a hymn, after which Jerry again speaks. He gives an invitation to all persons who are tired of sin and want to live a better life, and to all backsliders, to stand up and come forward towards the platform for prayers:

"We're going to have prayers now. Don't you want to be saved to-night? Who'll stand up for prayers? There's one; there's two; three; there's another! Don't be afraid to stand up. It don't make any difference what kind of clothes you've got on. Satan is telling some of you not to do it. He holds you back. I tell you Satan is no friend of yours. He goes round putting up all sorts of jobs on sinners; and he makes it pretty hot sometimes. You can't get the best of him! You've got to call upon the Lord for assistance if you want to get rid of your bad habits, and you've got to keep asking for it till he gives it. He won't be long about it. 'Ask and you shall receive,' is what he says. We need his help, every soul of us, great and small. When I see people who think themselves smart and cunning, dabbling in sin and forgetting God, I wonder they ain't suddenly snapped off, squelched just where they are! They all need help. Put 'em all in a bag—the rich sinners and the poor sinners—and shake 'em up, do you think there'd be any difference in 'em when they came out?

"You hear some people saying the Bible is a sham, and religion is all a hoax. Well, it may be to them, but it's God's power to me. Yes! Look at me, friends! Once I was a loafer and a rough. Never knew what it was to be contented and happy. Head on me like a mop; big scar across my nose all the time! I had an old red shirt, and a hat that looked as if it had been hauled up out of a tar-pot! If I had a coat, it was one of the kind with the cuffs up here to the elbows! split open in the back! Latest style! D'ye see? You couldn't find any drunken rowdy on the corner worse-looking than I was. I cursed God! I held up my hands and cursed him for giving me existence. Why had he put me in a hell on earth? Why had he made me a thief and a drunkard, while he gave other people wealth and pleasure? And then I suddenly thought that he had done none of those things. It was I that brought myself to what

I was! Yes, I did it myself! I made myself a drunkard
and a thief, and then went and accused God of it! Oh, God
is good, my friends! He is wise. He is merciful. If you
want common-sense—and who don't?—ask him for it!

"Some people say, 'Ah, I'm too bad; God wouldn't give
me a show.' That's all a mistake! He can save the vilest
sinner! God will take what the devil would almost refuse!
The very worst people are welcome to him. Didn't he save
the thief on the cross? I knew a man who came here into
this place to lick another for saying 'Jesus saves me.' Well,
Jesus saved that very man himself. He came looking for a
fight here, but the fight was all knocked out of him! God
did it. He went away like a cur trembling in a sack, and he
became a good Christian man, and he's a Christian now.
That's the way it is. Jesus is willing to save every one who
asks him honestly to do it.

"My friends, I want to tell you that it pays to serve
Jesus. He's a good friend. I used to hang round that rum-
shop on the corner; and they were glad enough to have me
there as long as my money lasted. But when that was gone
—'Jerry! take a walk! Take a walk around the block and
cool off!' I felt the insult down in my heart. It stung me.
But I couldn't help it; I was such a slave to my appetite.
I hadn't a friend in the world. But I can tell you it's not so
now! I have had friends and everything I need since I began to love and serve Jesus. Just look at me! Do I look
like a fraud now? I'm a new creature, inside and out!
I'm honest, I'm clean, and respected, and happy! Why,
those rich rum-sellers over there respect me now. They call
me Mister McAuley! 'Good-morning, Mr. McAuley!'
They are very polite! D'ye see? I can go into a bank
now, and the president will ask me into his private office,

while the big guns have to stand outside! 'Sit down; sir; what can I do for you?' And then he'll take me round and introduce me to the cashier! Ha! twelve years ago if he'd seen me coming into his bank he'd set the dogs on me, or send for a policeman to run me out! 'Fraid I'd steal all the money! Can't you see what the religion of Jesus has done for me? I tell you, the religion of Jesus makes a wonderful change in a man. I've got good friends, and a good home, and a good wife. And I've got money in my pocket, besides a clean heart full of joy and peace! The blessed Jesus has done it all. Do you want to know how to get those things? The Bible says how—'Seek first the kingdom of God and its righteousness, and all those things shall be added unto you.'

"There was a time when I'd cut a man's throat for a five-dollar bill, and kick him overboard! Do you suppose I'd do it now? Eh? Why not? 'Cause I've got the grace of God in my heart! Jesus saves me, and he can save any man. There's not a poor homeless fellow here to-night that isn't welcome to salvation. Jesus says, 'Him that cometh unto me I will in no wise cast out.' And the Bible says, 'He tasted death for every man.' Yes! Jesus died for every poor fellow that hasn't got any home or friends to-night! Won't you come to him and let him save you? Won't you come now?"

After this invitation some of the converts canvass the assembly and encourage every one to come forward for prayers who is inclined to do so, while all stand up and unite in singing a penitential hymn:

> "Just as I am—without one plea,
> But that Thy blood was shed for me,
> And that Thou bidd'st me come to Thee—
> O Lamb of God, I come."

All kneel down while one or two prayers are offered. Then each of the new-comers is asked to pray for himself. On such occasions fifteen or twenty poor miserable men may sometimes be seen on their knees—a position in which most of them were never seen before.

To the suggestion to pray for themselves some of them reply, " I can't !" " I don't know how !" " I never prayed in my life !" " I can't pray in English !" But when told that Jesus understands all languages, and that prayer is only asking him sincerely for what they most want, and that if the heart is right and honest the words are of little importance, because he looks at the heart and not at the lips, they exclaim, sometimes sobbing, " O God, save me !" " O God, have mercy upon me, a sinner !" " O God, take away my appetite for rum !" " O Jesus, I have been a very bad man. I want to do right; help me !" " O Lord, scratch out my sins, and keep them scratched out !" " Make my bed in heaven, O Lord !" " O Lord, forgive the past of my life ; and bless my aged mother to-night, who don't know where I am !"

Others, not knowing what to say, have repeated something which was taught them in childhood by religious parents. Evidences of early religious instruction are often revealed by the suppliants on these occasions—even by men who have become gray-haired in sin. Among the wretched men who for the first time prayed for themselves, was one who repeated the Lord's Prayer, another repeated a part of the Apostles' Creed, and another the infant's prayer, " Now I lay me down to sleep," etc.

These words—reminiscences of a time, long ago, when a loving mother watched over him and prayed for him—may be supposed to represent what the man in his penitence wanted to say, but did not know how.

The result of these meetings is thus constantly illustrating the truth that every man is a sinner, and that Jesus is the only Saviour, and that he is able and willing to save immediately the vilest wretch who comes, like the leper, "beseeching him, and kneeling down to him, and saying unto him, If thou wilt, thou canst make me clean" (Mark i. 40).

_____

It is gratifying to be able to record the fact that the Water Street meeting is still carried on. Souls are saved there constantly. It is one of many flourishing memorials of Jerry's redemption and consecration to Christ. It is no doubt true,

> " The evil that men do lives after them ;
> The good is oft interred with their bones."

But this is not always the case. Through God's mercy it is not so in the case of Jerry McAuley. There are very many souls, some in glory and others yet upon earth, who were led to Christ through his instrumentality. And this is not all, for, besides this, it is a blessed fact that the means and forces which he was permitted to put in operation for the salvation of lost men and women, remain and are still richly owned and blessed of God to that end.

CHAPTER XIX.

JERRY McAULEY'S CREMORNE MISSION.

"We sing the love that sought us,
We praise the blood that bought us,
We bless the grace that brought us
Back to the fold of God."

IN preceding pages, some account has been given of the change made by Jerry in his field of operations. Succeeding events have justified the step he took, although some of his best friends and most active coworkers did not advise it at the time, and indeed expressed themselves as doubting the wisdom of the change. They feared, no doubt, that the Water Street Mission would suffer, and possibly become extinct. But it was God's work, and God has taken care of it. Jerry was undoubtedly led of God to commence operations at No. 104 West Thirty-second Street, the location of the Cremorne Mission. Close to a crowded thoroughfare, and in a locality where sin openly abounds, such a beacon of warning is eminently in its place. From its first opening until the present time there has been an uninterrupted display of God's grace in saving power. Souls were saved at the very outset, and souls are being saved there now. Of course its earthly founder is missed; his presence, his testimony, his personal intercourse with men and women, his happy way of conducting the services, are no more; and in being deprived of these the Mission

14

has sustained a great loss, but the work had a heavenly Founder as well as an earthly one, and He remains.   His presence is still vouchsafed.   The voice of the Son of God is still heard, bringing the dead to life, speaking liberty to the bound, rest to the weary, hope and cheer to the hopeless, pardon to the penitent.

God uses means.   He is pleased to save souls through human instrumentalities, and when Jerry died the trustees in charge of the Mission realized that a superintendent must be appointed in his stead.   Many friends of the cause asked " Who can take his place ?"   To say that none could do so would be to limit the power of God to anoint souls for his work.   The trustees felt that God had the agent ready, and so sought wisdom and direction from above.   The result of their prayers and thought is well known.   From the very beginning of his mission-work Jerry had found a consecrated, cheerful, and able helper in the person of his wife.   To her the sacred trust, the conduct of the Mission, was committed; and God is blessing her labors and those of the many faithful and devoted helpers who seek to uphold her hands.   With the same deep love and hunger for souls that characterized her husband, with never-failing tact, with much of Jerry's gift of keen penetration into human nature, Mrs. McAuley labors to the utmost of her strength in her unremitting efforts to win the lost.   She gives her testimony in the meetings, as she has always done, often with tears in her own eyes, and often bringing tears to the eyes of her listeners.   She speaks frankly of her lost condition before Jesus saved her.   It is a sad story; she does not glory in it: far from that—it is with a pang of grief and with a sense of humiliation that she tells it.   But she feels as Jerry ever felt, that poor souls, hearing how she was lifted from the depths and so royally redeemed, will take heart, and be led to seek the same saving grace that she found. And it is just in this way that her testimony and the testimonies of others, given in the Mission meetings, are blessed. What more effective sermon could he whose eyes Christ opened have preached than this: " One thing I know, that whereas I was blind, now I see"? And the testimony uttered by so many, and so constantly owned of God to the salvation of souls in the Cremorne Mission, is just this: " I was lost, but now I am saved: Jesus has saved me."

In this connection, as showing that God's favor is still vouchsafed to the work, it will be in order to introduce the following sketch of the services at the Cremorne Mission. It was prepared by the writer at the time for *Jerry McAuley's Newspaper*, and is in its various features characteristic of the meetings in general. The sketch reports the service held on Sunday evening, November 9, 1884. It is copied in full.

A CREMORNE SUNDAY EVENING.

We have never attended a service in which the various parts blended more harmoniously or linked more completely than that of Sunday night, November 9, at the Cremorne Mission. The Holy Spirit was present in great power. There was no mere excitement, no froth, but a tidal-wave of blessing that carried us before it. Tears fell, for they could not be restrained. Strong men wept, and men and women smiled though their tears. So far as interest was concerned, there was not a dull minute. In view of the packed hall, we were led to wonder why ministers should complain of the difficulty of getting a Sabbath-evening audience—as many ministers do complain. People come here, people of all classes, and from various quarters of the city. As usual on Sunday evenings, many friends were compelled to stand, yet one seat was vacant: the chair of the departed missionary, Jerry McAuley, has never been occupied since his death. It stands upon the platform in the old place. We have no veneration for wood, but that empty chair, with its drapery of black, speaks volumes sometimes. Yes, the vacant chair has a voice—hark to its words of warning, " Be ye also ready!" Hark to its word of encouragement, " Be thou faithful unto death and I will give thee a crown of life."

After the service of song, prayer was offered and the fifty-fifth chapter of Isaiah was read by the leader, Mr. Corning. This is the chapter that opens with the call to the thirsty to buy and eat without money and without price. With exemplary brevity, the leader spoke of the rich blessings enjoyed here on past occasions, and called for testimonies from those who accepted Christ as their Saviour.

" I am glad that I am able and willing and anxious to speak for Jesus," said the first. " Seven or eight years ago He was precious to my soul, and I enjoyed His love. Then an evil spirit seemed to take possession of me. I fell away, and became addicted to the use of strong drink. Through this I was separated from my wife and children. I came to New York, and when the past rose up before me, as it often would, I would drink to drown the memories. I met a brother, brother M——, over there, and he brought me to his house. Then he brought me to this Mission. Each testimony I heard here struck me hard. I went forward to those chairs, but I did not get satisfied that night, and I fell back again. A few days ago I met brother M—— again, and he induced me to come here, and I went again as a seeker to those chairs. There was a great void in me until then, but I rejoice to be able to tell you that the void is filled. The love of Christ has filled it. I rejoice in him to-night."

One of the hymns we had sung, "Walk in the light," etc., brought another to his feet. Last night, on his way home from the Florence Mission, he met with drunken men lying in dark corners of the streets—their only sleeping-place. This brought to his mind his former condition. Before that light of which we had been singing dawned on him he had often slept in just such corners. He had long been a slave of strong drink. "Now," he added, "I look up and thank God that I am walking in the light, 'the beautiful light of God.'" The light had been growing brighter all along. God had taught him how to sing and to speak, to watch and pray. "Pray God," he said, "to show me other poor drunkards that I may go to and speak about Jesus."

Brother M——, referred to by the first friend who testified, twice essayed to speak but was prevented first by another testimony, then by the call for the singing of a hymn. "The devil," he said, "tempted me to keep quiet, when I was twice prevented from speaking, but I would not let him beat me that way. I did everything I could when that brother who spoke first was serving God, years ago, to lead him to ruin. We were old friends. We were in the fire-department together, and in the army together, and, I may say, we went through the mill together. So it was not to be wondered at that I should seek to have him saved. I am so happy; God has saved my soul from hell, and I wanted him saved too. After we left the Mission last night he did not feel as though God had forgiven him his sin.

To-night four of us went up into the gallery before the time for this service had come, and there we prayed that he might confess Christ to-night; and he has done it."

There was something very touching about this incident. The joy of the one friend at having the deep void in his heart filled was so evident, that it was contagious. But when we heard of brother M——'s deep anxiety for his old associate's conversion, and then of this little gallery prayer-meeting, and saw the prompt response vouchsafed of God, our hearts were deeply affected. We recalled the four men who brought their palsied friend to Jesus, and whose faith was so honored of the Master. A sense of holy awe fell upon the meeting. We felt that that gracious Saviour was most assuredly present through his Holy Spirit.

> " No man can truly say
>   That Jesus is the Lord,
> Unless thou take the veil away
>   And breathe the living Word."

The veil had been removed, and so we knew that the Holy Spirit was at work among us. We realized the words:

> "——heaven comes down our souls to greet,
>   And glory crowns the mercy-seat."

The next speaker had known the Lord for several years. He meets with adversaries at his daily toil. They ask him why he believes in God when he cannot see any God. He tells them that when at sea he steered by the compass, though he could not see the land to which it pointed, and thus steering he reached the port in safety. So since he had steered by God's Word he had known peace and joy although he had not seen God face to face.

"I know whom I have put my trust in," said another;

"it is Jesus Christ. Many a time I have said to Jerry McAuley, 'Mr. McAuley, I mean, by the grace of God, to keep in this way.' He would say, 'My boy, hold on to Christ.' Now he has fought and won, but he is not out of sight altogether; I shall meet him again."

"I can praise God to-night. How I do praise him for answering my prayer for mercy ten months ago!" another said.

We sang from the hymn—

> "Let the lower lights be burning,
> Send a gleam across the wave," etc.,

when a convert said, "That illustrates my case. If there had not been a light in Thirty-second Street I should probably have been in perdition now. Until I came here, eighteen months ago, my wife and family were heart-broken. I was a drunkard, and when I came home my wife did not know whether to expect a kind word or a blow. This went on for eighteen years. It seemed as if there was something down in perdition drawing me there. Rum had so much the best of me that I had lost my will. How many fights with the devil I had! Eighteen months ago I came here and was saved; now I am able to say 'no' when tempted to do wrong."

"I thought I was as good as anybody until, as I came to this meeting, I discovered I was as bad as anybody," was the testimony of one who added, "I want to keep my light low that others may see it. My prayer is that God may keep me humble and honest."

The next speaker came to pay a farewell visit to the Mission. About two years and a half ago, as he and an associate walked along Sixth Avenue, he said to his friend, "John, come along and let us see what kind of a place tney have got here," meaning the Mission.   He came, and to tell the story in his own words, "I came five times and I was convicted of sin.   I saw I was in the wrong way, yet I was not willing to surrender to Jesus.   Two years and seven months ago I knelt down at those chairs, and sought and found mercy.   Further on, the Lord called me out to work for him, and now I am bound for the Congo.   I leave next Saturday with a band of missionaries.   Pray God to use us for the salvation of precious souls."   It was on an Easter Sunday that the speaker first found peace with God through our Lord Jesus Christ.

At this point a verse of Hymn No. 72, in Gospel Praise Book, was called for, and sung with much fervor:

> " Behold the changing autumn leaves,
>   Behold the fields of ripening grain,
> Go gather in the golden sheaves,
>   From valley, hill, and distant plain.
>
> " Then reapers haste, the skies are clear,
>   The fields resound the glad refrain,
> The harvesters from far and near,
>   Are gathering in the golden grain."

"I wish that brother God speed," said Mrs. McAuley, "but he won't find a blacker heart in all Africa than mine was in this city of New York before Jesus saved me over fifteen years ago, and he has kept me ever since.   Pray God to bless this brother in Africa and to bless me here."

A brother said he had been impressed with a hymn sung at the church service which he attended in the morning, "If I've Jesus, only Jesus."   It was such a comfort to him to know that he could take Jesus to his work with him in the morning. For nearly fourteen years he had found a friend in Jesus. The speaker commended the decision of the young brother who was going to Africa. Missionaries did good. He remembered a missionary in Hong Kong whose words had produced a deep impression on him. The brother had a very happy experience when he was saved. Previous to his finding peace it seemed as though hell were just ready to swallow him up. It was eight o'clock one morning when he realized he was saved. For twelve days after that he hardly knew whether he was in the body or out, because of Christ's wonderful peace and joy in his soul.

That same peace and joy has been experienced by another who told something of what grace had done for him. "There are no limits to the power of Christ to save," he said; "a little over thirty years ago I was with a bad crowd in California. I learned the tricks that are vain. I knew I was doing wrong, and I was on the wrong path until nearly five years ago. Then I resolved to change my course of life and I did it with an earnestness that God honored. Jerry gave me the text, 'Seek ye first the kingdom of God and his righteousness, and all these things shall be added unto you.' I had schemed and planned and troubled a good deal to get these very things which God promised to give if I would obey him. I resolved from that moment out to test God's promise. I took a good letter to Mr. H—— (then the head of a large dry-goods establishment), but he dismissed me rudely, and when I left him the old nature began boiling up. Then I said to myself, 'This is not what I promised God.' Presently as I was going down the Bowery I met an old associate, who unfolded a little scheme. He wanted me to take part in it, and my share in the transaction would have yielded me $40 in twenty minutes. But I told him I had made a promise to God and I would stick to it if I starved, so I could not have anything more to do with such schemes. Then I met a broker who had given me many points, and he never gave me any information that I failed on when I used it. But I told him that I did not want to hear any of his points. I went on to the Water Street Mission, and sister McAuley gave me a day's work. I scrubbed the floor and cleaned the windows of the Mission. When I got through she said they were done better than ever she had had them done. Well, I had prayed God to instruct me as I did the work. Now I am doing well; God sent me a friend who put me into business, lending me money. I am prospering, and hope to be out of debt by next spring. From my experience I can say, ' Put your trust in God: he'll honor it.' One Sunday evening a woman called for a dress my wife was making for her. The dress was not quite finished, for the buttons had to be sewn on. The customer wanted my wife to complete the work there and then; but she would not do it because it was Sunday. Then the woman was angry and called my wife a thief, saying she believed the dress had been pawned. She then left, but next morning she came in again. She lived in Brooklyn, but had stayed in New York at a friend's house all night. She expressed her sorrow for her conduct on the previous day, got her dress, and paid six dollars for it. We found then, as we have ever since, that God's providences will come in when they are needed. I have grown in faith since I first started in this way."

Until twenty-two years old, a gentleman said, he had been without God, being utterly ignorant of the Bible, never having read it an hour in his life. Then he was persuaded to seek the Lord. God opened his eyes and while he saw he was a sinner he saw also that he was the very sinner Christ came into the world to save. For threescore years and three he had been a Christian and Jesus had proved more and more precious to him. It was grand to hear this veteran talk of the peace with God, the peace of soul, the absence of anxiety, and forgiveness, and the blessed consciousness of sin forgiven, and of a title to life eternal which he enjoyed. He commended this religion of Christ, and concluded with the statement that there had been too much testimony given that night to be neglected.

A solemn thought was presented by another: it was the close proximity of the living and the dead. In these seats sat the saved and the unsaved. This Mission place was God's house; the place next door below might well be characterized as hell. So there was many a one here to-night in whose heart there was heaven, while there was a very hell in the heart that beat next to him, but God's Word was, "He that hath the Son hath life," and those now lost had but a step to take to make Christ theirs and so take heaven for hell. Some might fear to accept Christ and start in the Christian way because they wondered how they could be Christians amid the temptations of life. But to those who believe in Christ God gives the power to become sons. "I cannot tell you how he does it," said the speaker; "he takes away the stony heart and gives us a new heart. He has given me fifteen years of this life, in which I have had more peace and joy than I can ever tell."

A sister said it was two years and over since she realized that God had forgiven her sins. She had had much forgiven. Addicted to the use of a strong and poisonous drug, she had gone far towards destroying herself. Indeed, the physicians told her that she had but six months to live. It was when in this sad state that she was laid under conviction of sin and

turned to the Lord Jesus Christ. He saved her, and destroyed the power of her awful appetite. He forgave her sins
and healed her body. She then resolved to consecrate herself to the Lord, and she thought he would surely lead her
into some Missionary service. But no: the way opened into
a kitchen, with cooking and washing and ironing to be done.
This was a strange, mysterious Providence. Friends told
her she was wasting her time, but she said she believed the
Lord had put her there. At this work she proposed to stay
till the Lord opened a way out. This the Lord had now
done; she, too, was about to start for Africa, and she had
reason to know that the domestic acts which she had been
learning would make her useful in her new field of labor.

A young man told us that two years ago he came here to
transact some business with Jerry McAuley. As he sat here
and heard what was said he became convicted of sin and then
sought forgiveness of God through the Lord Jesus Christ.

All along the Christian's religion had been presented in
glowing colors. The friends who spoke bore abundant evidence that to have the grace of Christ Jesus in the heart was
to have a treasure indeed. In view of this there was great
force in the words of a young brother, who, after telling us
that God had saved him too, added, " and all this we got
without money and without price." Great indeed is the
wealth of the Christian inheritance—priceless in value yet
offered without price.

After the testimonies, an earnest appeal was made to the
unsaved to make this the night of their surrender to Christ.
" Do not wait for feeling: it is the devil's trick to destroy
souls, to make you wait for feeling," the speaker said. He
then recited some thrilling incidents that were told in a way
not to be forgotten. By each incident some point was

emphasized, and the address was most solemn, tender, and earnest. When the opportunity was afforded, a number of persons raised the hand to signify that they wished to start on the Christian life and that they desired prayer. Thus the first service was brought to a close. We rejoice to know that some left the place rejoicing in the knowl-edge of their newly-found Lord and Saviour. The angels had work to do in " bearing the tidings home," and there was joy in heaven as well as on earth, for heaven makes merry over the salvation of the lost.

Some years have passed since this record was made, but the meetings continue with unabated interest: the prayer of the penitent is still heard, wanderers are reclaimed, back-sliders are restored, and God's free grace revealed in Christ is glorified. Here, too, those who are moralists, and know not Christ's presence in the heart, are convicted of their need of his salvation. The respectable and the ragged, the self-righteous and the sinner, bow side by side at the throne of grace, and are brought to know the Lord Jesus as a personal Saviour.

CHAPTER XX.

JERRY AS A JOURNALIST AND CORRESPONDENT.

"God's grace will to the end
  Stronger and brighter shine ;
Nor present things, nor things to come,
  Shall quench the love divine."

IN June, 1883, Jerry began the publication of a bi-weekly journal, which he entitled *Jerry McAuley's Newspaper.* Published every other Thursday, it was Jerry's idea that it should contain reports of the meetings at the Cremorne Mission, giving the pith of the testimonies there uttered, and also records of other city mission-work. The paper is still issued, Mrs. McAuley feeling that she could not allow her husband's cherished project to fail. It is dependent for its financial support upon the annual subscriptions of friends and the advertising patronage of a number of well-known business men who are deeply interested in its welfare. Many copies of each issue are sent to inmates of prisons, penitentiaries, and other institutions. Some of those who have read in their prison-cells the testimonies of former convicts at the Mission, have been led upon their own release to come there for themselves, and to seek and find the Saviour of the lost. Some indeed, through God's blessing upon the printed pages, have while yet incarcerated been moved to confess their sins to God, and implore divine pardon. Thus while prisoners of the law of man they have become free men in Christ Jesus. The paper has been distributed among the sick in hospitals, and in some instances the dying have learned from its columns the way of life, and have entered thereupon. Many earnest Christian workers both near and far have testified to the encouragement to faith derived from the reading of this journal. In moments of depression, when the difficulties in connection with their service for Christ seemed many and almost insurmountable, or when they wearily watched for fruit that seemed long coming, they have read the records of God's work at the Cremorne or some kindred mission, and have found their love for the Master's service warmed and their zeal inspired afresh.

It was Jerry's hope that his "Newspaper" might be accorded such a hearty support that the profits might ere long permit of the establishment of a Home for erring but penitent sisters. Here he proposed such should find a refuge from their lives of evil, while seeking avenues of honorable employment. Jerry died without realizing this wish, but bequeathed his desire and hope to Mrs. McAuley, who cherishes the same design.

The journal is still conducted in accordance with Jerry's views. It presents the saving truths of the Gospel in an attractive form, and it is the conviction of those who most regularly peruse its contents, that the paper succeeds in the high aim of its editors, which is to "preach Christ Jesus, and Him crucified, on every page."

Without this reference to a work which was so dear to Jerry's heart this memorial volume would be incomplete. The "Newspaper" still bears Jerry's name, and it is a constant memorial of God's grace as manifested in him. It also carries hither and thither the glad story of Christ's saving grace and power as proclaimed by men and women who, like Jerry, have been brought out of the horrible pit and the miry clay, but whose feet have been placed upon the rock eternal, in whose mouth, as in his, has been placed the new song, even praise unto our God. They sing that song on earth, he sings it before the throne. Yet it is the same song—the song of Moses and the Lamb, the song of redeeming love.

Jerry's early life deprived him of the advantages of education ; and from this fact, and possibly in part from his very active disposition, he had no love for correspondence. Few specimens of his handwriting in any shape are in existence ; but while at Sing Sing he dictated some letters, a few of which are in the possession of a lady in this city. Jerry makes grateful mention of this lady and the Christian service she rendered him, as will be seen in Chapter I., page 18, where he speaks of her as Miss D——; and through her kindness we have been permitted to read these letters and to publish two of them. These letters show that before his release Jerry's spiritual life was very real. It is evident that he fed much upon God's Word. No doubt he there studied it very thoroughly, and laid large portions of its contents up in store. From that store he drew copiously in the after-days, for in his addresses and his comments upon Scripture he showed great familiarity with the Book. His expositions of Scripture, always quaint and original, bore witness that he had reached the heart of the matter.

Two of the letters are appended. The first was written to a good sister in Christ—an old lady in one of our public almshouses; the second was addressed to the friend already mentioned.

SING SING, Feb. 3, 1863.

DEAR SISTER: I received your kind letter, and read it with pleasure. I do assure you I am unworthy of your Christian love. I thank you, dear friend, for your kind sympathy for me in my present misfortune. You spoke of some little refreshments that I sent you. I don't remember sending you anything. I gave something to the friend that wrote your letter, and told her to give it to whom she pleased. I gave it cheerfully, because my Heavenly Father put it in my heart to do so; therefore you must thank the kind Friend who gave you those little comforts. I wish I had something worth sending; I would do so very cheerfully, but the time may come when I can do so.

You ask me to continue in prayer. My dear sister, I could not sleep nor eat without prayer. Prayer is the only source of comfort that the true Christian enjoys. Those are good hymns that you speak of. I have got two of them at heart. One of them is " Jesus, lover of my soul." The other is " Prayer is the soul's sincere desire." I am very thankful to you for your prayers, and hope that they will be answered. You will continue to pray for me. I do indeed feel for you in your misfortunes, but feeling will not help you. I do rejoice now that you love the Lord Jesus so much. The friend who wrote to you told me about you, and spoke very highly of you. She has promised to take me to see you when I get out. But my hopes are discouraging now, because my friends have not proceeded as I wished they should; but there is no use talking now. It troubled me when I heard of it; but, dear sister, if we do not meet on earth, I hope we shall in heaven. The day I received your letter, that night I knelt down and prayed that God would spare your life until I saw you. I had that

15

sweet assurance that my heavenly Father heard my prayer. I love to read my Bible.   I have got by heart the following chapters: Timothy 6th; Hebrews 11th and 12th; James 1st; Luke 24th; Psalms 34, 51, 88, 90, 91, 103, 119, and 143.   I have got a great many texts, but I will not mention them. I have said nothing on spiritual things.   I know that I love my dear Lord Jesus.   I feel happy lately.

Now I must bid you a good-by.   Give my Christian regards to all who love the Lord Jesus.

Yours in Christ,   JERRY McAULEY.

SING SING, May 11, 1863.

MISS D——.

DEAR FRIEND: I received your kind letter, which was the source of great comfort to me.   I found in it sweet Christian counsel; all your letters have been the means of cheering me in my sad moments.   I wish you would write to me often, if you feel disposed to do so.

I read a chapter in the Bible this morning: it was John 16th: "Verily I say unto you, that ye shall weep and lament, but the world shall rejoice; and ye shall be sorrowful, but your sorrow shall be turned into joy."   This verse struck me forcibly, and made a deep impression on me.   I think a great deal upon our last interview, especially about Abraham.   You must not think for a moment that I am ungrateful for the many favors you so generously bestowed upon me.   I feel indeed that I can never repay this debt of gratitude.   Your sweet Christian advice has given me some encouragement, but I leave all things in the hands of my heavenly Father.   He will do all things right.

Dear sister, it is my desire that you would pray much for

me   I never wanted them more.   Give my kind Christian regards to Mrs. L——; also remember me to Miss H——. Tell her that I am very glad that she is getting well.

Yours truly,   JERRY MCAULEY.

———

Our task is accomplished.   To God the source of all real good, who alone can make this volume a blessing to its readers, it is committed, with the ardent prayer that he will use it for his glory.   Amen.

———

NOTE.—The pictures of Mr. and Mrs. McAuley contained in this book are from plates executed by the "Photo-Electrotype Engraving Company," 20 Cliff Street, from the excellent negatives taken by the well-known photographer Mr. Charles D. Fredericks, 770 Broadway, New York.

THE END.